ENEMY COUNTRY

Emilio DeGrazia

ENEMY COUNTRY

Emilio DeGrazia

New Rivers Press 1984

Library of Congress Catalog Card Number: 84-060334
ISBN 089823-055-1
Typesetting: Peregrine Cold Type
Book design: Daren Sinsheimer
Cover by Caroline Garrett

Earlier versions of these stories appeared in the following publications:
"The Enemy" in *North Country Anvil*; "The Mask" in *Green River Review*;
"The Girl and the Two Old Men" in *Colorado Quarterly*; "The Death of
Sin" in *Carleton Miscellany*; "Enemy Country" (as "Gooks") in *Touchstone*;
"The Sniper" in *Samizdat*. "The Brothers of the Tiger" was anthologized
in *Likely Stories*, edited by Bruce McPherson and published by Treacle
Press (1981). Special thanks to Bruce McPherson for permission to photo-
stat charts, graphs, and other special material used in "Brothers to the
Tiger." Special thanks also to Susan Roberts for providing useful critical
comments and to Monica Dreslan, who has been a steady and generous
source of encouragement, and to Caroline Garrett for designing the covers
of this book, and to Terry Schwarze for providing technical assistance on
the cover.

Publication of *Enemy Country* was made possible in part by grants from the
National Endowment for the Arts (with funds provided by the Congress of
the United States) and by the United Arts Council (with funds provided in
part by the McKnight Foundation).

New Rivers Press books are distributed by

Bookslinger   and   Small Press Distribution
213 East 4th St.   1784 Shattuck Ave.
St. Paul, MN   Berkeley, CA
55101   94709

Enemy Country had been manufactured in the United States of America for
New Rivers, Inc. (C. W. Truesdale, editor/publisher), 1602 Selby Ave., St.
Paul, MN 55104 in a first edition of 2000 copies.

The kittens kept asking the cat if he had ever been to the land where the tigers roamed.

The cat did not like to say yes or no.

"How do you *know*, then, if there really were tigers in that land? How do you *know*?"

"I know in my own way," the cat replied, "just as you know in your own way. For in our day we all have been there, and still are."

ENEMY COUNTRY

ENEMY COUNTRY

THE DEATH OF SIN

The four soldiers were as confused about who was responsible for the death of Sin as they were about the accident of war that brought them together.

"One day she was here, that's all," said Lund, "and now she's gone. It's like getting drafted. There but for fortune go you and I," he told Robinson, Dorner, and Cowgill, the other three privates he was always seen with after the four of them survived an ambush in the bush. "We'll never get another dog like that," he added. The others, their faces hanging, agreed.

Dogs like Sin did not come along every day. There were other dogs on the base, but they were German Shepherds trained to find the enemy. The big dogs were all business. "Not the kind of dog you take home to Mom," remarked Robinson. When one day Lieutenant Colonel Otterby ordered twelve of them shot because they took off after some rabbits instead of Viet Cong, no one seemed to mind.

But Sin was different. One day she just appeared on the road outside the messhall, sitting precariously on one haunch and looking up serenely out of sad brown eyes at the four privates who gathered around. She was a small mutt lost in a swirl of fur that was neither brown nor yellow, and as she sat looking up at the soldiers she never spoke or whined, even when Lund put his hand on her broken hind leg.

The next day at noon they met Lund and the mutt outside the messhall again, the mutt looking shinier this time and her leg as strong as the splint Lund had made from a stick ripped off an orange crate. "Her name is Sin," Lund announced to the other three. "Take one look at that little devil's face and you'll see what I mean." But they knew there was more to the name than that. "Tell the truth," Dorner said. "She reminds you of that yellow whore in Saigon—the one that wore you out, the one with the limp."

"Which one?" Lund asked with innocent eyes.

So she became known as Sin, with Lund her acknowledged master and the other three her guardians. Lund had the clearest right to her be-

9

cause he had seen her first. "And because he's got a college degree," said Dorner with a jeer, "in sociology." Yet they all shared her as equally as they shared the fate that had brought them together, an ambush that left them all shamelessly afraid but alive. It was the fear that had made them a group despite their differences. If Dorner, the dark one from Idaho, complained about the food, Robinson, a bitter pug-faced Huck Finn from Ohio, complained about Dorner's complaining. And when Cowgill, an insurance crop-adjuster from Alabama, spoke about chasing girls at ski resorts in Colorado, Lund rambled on about farming again with his father in Minnesota. Thus their thoughts went their own ways, even though they were seen together so often that some of the other soldiers began calling them "The Group."

The dog, rather than the fear, kept them together. They had found an orphan, not like the ones they had seen in the streets of Saigon but like the ordinary mutts they had left behind like childhoods in their home towns.

So they began caring for Sin. Outside of Lund's barracks they cut a door in an overturned crate and filled the crate with a bed of grass. Every day they brought scraps of meat back with them from the messhall and laid them before her like a burnt offering, and she, like a haughty queen, turned up her nose at the gift until they were out of sight. By the time she was able to limp without her splint, most of the men on the base knew her by name, just as they knew of the regulation forbidding pets.

One afternoon the dog wandered away to the spot in the middle of the road where she had first appeared, and when the group saw her she was sitting like a monk waiting for the end of time. For a moment the group thought that Sin's time had come. For out of a dust cloud down the road came Otterby's jeep at forty miles an hour. Without moving a haunch the dog opened an eye and turned her head to face the commotion, just as Lund closed his eyes and waited for the end. The end was noisier than he imagined, for Otterby's jeep swerved into some garbage cans to keep from hitting her. If the jeep didn't get her, Lund thought before opening his eyes, Otterby would order her shot. As all four watched Otterby march a dazed line from the garbage cans to the dog, they resisted the urge to rush onto the road, scoop the dog under an arm, and disappear into the bush beyond the base. They were sure—if the expression on Otterby's face was any clue— that he would have executed her right there on the road had he not seen everyone watching him. As his eyes met the group's his pace slackened and a change like a smile of approval spread over his face. When he bent down and stroked the mutt on the head they let a little cheer go up, and Otterby answered with an informal salute in their direction.

They knew then that Sin was theirs to keep, even before Otterby called them over to ask them how she had appeared on the road.

"OK, then," he said, "you can take care of it, but you'll have to keep it chained up. We can't let a bunch of dogs run loose around here."

Because they did tie her up to the crate they couldn't understand how she got loose two weeks later and therefore got killed.

"Goddammit," said Robinson a week after it happened. "I'd like to know whose fault it was."

"Well you can't blame the dog either," said Lund. "She was just sitting on her spot."

"I'd like to know who untied her," said Dorner.

They all turned to Lund.

"Maybe she just got loose by herself," said Lund.

"You say she wasn't dead when they took her over to the hospital?" asked Robinson.

"I wouldn't send a gook over there," said Dorner.

"Well, that's that." Robinson lowered his eyes.

"And it's too damn bad," said Cowgill. "In fact it's a damn shame. When I came back here from the bush I used to look forward to seeing her. She'd be one of the first things I'd go see. And sure enough, she'd be waiting for me as faithful as a wife."

The three of them turned with angry eyes toward Lund.

II

Lieutenant Colonel Frank Otterby leaned back in his chair and expelled a deep breath as he stared at the desk calendar he had just flipped. Only two words—"report" and "Willy"—stared back at him. "And I've got to take care of them both this morning," he told himself, "so I can be free the rest of the day."

He felt no urge to reread the memo that had reached his desk the day before. It was short enough to memorize and disturbing enough to be closed away with a pile of other papers in the bottom drawer of his desk. In plain words it ordered him to file a report explaining who was to blame for the mistake made over the village outside Nha Trang. Two sentences: the second one ordered him to complete the report within a week.

He stared at the calendar for a long minute before drawing himself back to the desk. In a half hour he would have to face Willy, the cook who would not take no for an answer. "I could get the report done before then," he thought, "and then I could tell him to go to hell."

He poured himself a cup of coffee and turned to the window. To his right the landing strip, lined with Phantoms that looked like insects standing at attention, receded from him and dissolved into the soft glare of the morning sun, and to his left barracks stood in suburban rows against a mountain that rose like a green wall between him and a yellow haze he had always seen on horizons in this land.

"So what is there to explain." he thought, "What is there to report?

Someone gave an order, and someone else executed it. And in this case the results were not right." For a moment his mind flashed back to him the face of Norman, the crew-cut soldier who had flown the reconnaisance mission over the village. After he bailed out over the jungle on the way back, Norman was found days later hanging in a tree, his head encased in a bamboo cage into which the V. C. had placed a living rat. "So what is there to explain?" he said as he turned back to his desk.

He took out a blank sheet of paper and placed it before himself on the desk. "Human or mechanical. There are two factors—men and machines— and they can go wrong." He did not write the words but spoke them aloud as if to test their sound, even as other words came to him. "Somehow or other this plane went wrong," he thought, "and a village was bombed. People are sad, but they accept this is war and these things happen. There is no animosity. I'd like to say I'm sorry, but how can you say you're sorry?" Even as they formed in his mind he knew he could not write these words. No one wanted to hear this. Headquarters wanted someone to be responsible.

Without writing a word he turned to the window again, and until a knock broke the silence he did not turn back to face his desk. Even before Willy was shown in Otterby had put the report out of mind. Before him stood the son of an Italian immigrant, a short dark private who ruled the kitchen with a big wooden spoon. Each day as the food was served Willy stood over a huge potful of soup with the spoon and waved orders at the men filing by. He was eccentric enough to plot nine months of guerrilla warfare on a cat lurking nights around his kitchen, and clever enough to get his prey, just as he was smart enough to get Lincoln Jones, a black private from Chicago, transferred to another unit because Jones had found a hair in Willy's soup and complained. Everyone knew that Willy, though only a private, ran the kitchen, because they could see angry pride in his eyes challenging anyone to complain as he stood over the day's soup. He told the men he was the only one looking out for them, and he told them they ought to be grateful.

But few except Otterby knew how Willy managed to make the food come out so good. He did not supervise the menu or cook anything but the soup. He seemed like nothing more than a dark errand boy whose main job was to carry to the kitchen the raw material that the cooks turned into the stuff of life. But he winked at soldiers when they saw him unloading the trucks at the rear of the messhall. "Wait 'til you see what we eat tomorrow," he bragged in a whisper.

What Otterby knew was that Willy could get from him what the chief cook could not. About once every two weeks Willy came with a request which he called a "need." "Sir, I have a need, sir. Tenderloin for next Saturday night," he once announced to Otterby. "We know where there's some, and we know how you can pay for it." Otterby gave him only a sideways glance before Willy went on. "Gasoline. You get ten thousand less gallons this week. That's all. You don't need it anyway and you'll have some left over to spend."

Otterby responded to this with another sideways glance, but the men had tenderloin that Saturday and ate like princes at least once a week after that. And no one, not even the bespectacled accountant, missed the gasoline.

But Willy had gone too far. The men were boasting of Willy's cuisine to outsiders, and it was becoming suspect. "How do you get time to fight on food like that?" a visiting general once asked Otterby. "Makes you want to read a book and doze off."

So when Willy finally came out with it this time, Otterby had to say no. "Legs of lamb? Eight hundred legs of lamb? Will you drive to Australia yourself, and round up a couple hundred lambs? The answer is no, Willy. Absolutely no."

"But we can manage, sir," Willy pleaded. "I'm not asking for money, or special favors. We know where we can get them. I only need permission for a truck and some cover off-base."

"The answer is no, Willy. We can't do these things. Things go wrong sometimes, Willy, and then I'm to blame."

"But if nothing goes wrong sir, and no one's to blame? Then can I get the legs?"

"You'll get no permission for a truck and cover off-base, and that's final. If you can make the legs walk out of the sky like manna, I'll eat one gladly. But things around here will have to be done according to regulation. And that, Willy, is final."

III

Someone who saw it happen said that Sin didn't even wince when she became aware of the truck bearing down on her. "She looked like one of those Buddhist monks just sitting there like there was nothing she could do, but thinking it would turn out all right anyway. She would have passed right under the truck and come out the other end okay if she just would have ducked."

"And now she's nothing but a pile of garbage."

"It's my fault," said Cowgill.

"No, it's not your fault. I'm not sure I checked the leash when I left her last night," said Lund.

"But I saw her this morning, and I didn't check the leash," said Dorner.

"I think we're all to blame. None of us bothered to check the leash," said Cowgill.

"Because we didn't want her tied up, that's why. We all wanted her to run free around here like some gook's wild teenage daughter. I think we got what we deserved," said Dorner.

"Goddammit," said Robinson.

"But who in the hell was driving the truck? That's what I'd like to know. He didn't even slow down."

"But he stopped. He said it was his fault," said Cowgill. "He said he didn't see her until it was too late."

"Well, there's nothing you can do now. It's just one of those things."

"Oh shut up," someone said to Lund.

"Next thing you know we'll be blaming the dog. We've only got ourselves to blame."

"I feel like she was my own sister."

"Oh shut up, you make me sick."

"Goddammit, all of you shut up."

Without looking at each other they all turned away from the dog's remains when they heard Willy shouting at them from the top step of the messhall. "Get that thing out of here. People who walk by here have to eat." He waved at them menacingly with his big wooden spoon, and Lund bent down to lift the dead dog into his arms.

IV

Otterby had filed his report before Willy came in a second time to request a truck for the legs of lamb. He had typed the report himself, weighing each word scribbled in a longhand first draft. Then he revised his draft three times, each time cutting out words until the whole report amounted to three one-sentence paragraphs. "They're interested in conclusions, not explanations," he reasoned as his pen cut through sentences like a terrible swift sword. "I could have said it all in one sentence," he said to himself. "An order was sent to me, one of my men was sent to execute it, and a mistake was made. And that's all there is to it." He looked at the final typed version with some pride. It was clear, concise, and correct.

The strange phone call came after Willy tried a second time. "Sir, our need is for a truck," said Willy. "We have the legs. We only need a truck."

"Isn't all the food trucked in here?" Otterby's words had teeth in them. "We get food trucks running in and out of here every day. What's wrong with one of them? Why do you have to have one of our trucks?"

"It's part of the deal, sir. We already have the legs. But they said we'd have to pick them up in our truck." Willy's left eye twitched.

"What kind of deal is that? Is it a regular deal?"

"It's in the books, sir."

Otterby stared hard at Willy, whose face and body had stiffened to attention. Then he relaxed into his chair. "It isn't done," he said. "You'll have to call this one off. I can't have my trucks coming and going for legs of

14

lamb. Suppose one of them gets hit? Then I'm to blame. Then it's my fault. No. A mistake has been made already. I can't afford another one. I've got to take care of my men."

After Willy left, Otterby found himself in front of the window gazing at the runway at the far end of the base. The Phantoms had all left, and nothing remained but a haze still lingering in the late morning air. He had not heard them leave and remembered them in rows saluting with their wings. "A review," Otterby thought, "someday I'll have a review. I'll have them all line up—men and machines—and I'll have them pass in review. We don't do enough of that kind of thing these days."

The thought passed through him like a dream, losing itself between the space where he stood and the empty runway in the distance. He heard nothing, even as he turned to put the telephone receiver to his ear. As the small voice began speaking, he suppressed a yawn.

"Your report is unacceptable. You will have to resubmit."

Unacceptable. His heart leaped, even as the word turned into a blank as white as a sheet of paper.

"It is required in two days."

"By whom is this order given?"

"Headquarters. It is not another report requested. The same report is required. Do you understand?"

He did not understand—until later that day.

"And do you have carbons or copies of the original?"

Again he did not understand.

"No, I don't. I had none made."

"I see you understand then."

V

No one saw Otterby until late afternoon the next day. No one saw him leave his office after he received the phone call, and some say he spent the night there. His assistant had been ordered not to disturb him, and within hours rumors began drifting about the base.

"Troubles. With his wife," said Dorner.

"More trouble with his wife?"

"They say he went home one day and caught her in bed with a private."

"I would have killed the sonofabitch."

"Why him?"

"They say Otterby almost killed *her*."

"He should have."

"He was probably drunk. They say he drinks too much."

"They found him dead drunk one night—curled up asleep on top of his desk, papers and all, like a cat."

15

"He's being moved up," said Cowgill.

"No, down," said Lund.

"It's ending. This stupid goddam war is ending," said Robinson.

"If it doesn't, it ain't my fault. They didn't ask me about how to run it," said Lund.

All night Otterby, locked in his office, asked himself what head-quarters wanted, and the next day there were no sounds except a pacing back and forth and occasional bursts on the typewriter. Finally, right after the sun fell behind the green mountain beyond the landing strip, Otterby, unshaven and wearing a worn smile, emerged.

"Is there anything that needs to be done before I retire for the night?" he asked his assistant.

"Sir. Just the usual forms to be signed. And the private was here from the messhall again. Willy, the one from the kitchen, sir. He said it was ur-gent to get your signature today for one of their operations. He waited half the morning and all afternoon, even though I told him you would not be disturbed. He made me promise I'd mention it to you."

"What kind of operation?"

"A necessary purchase, sir. That's what he said."

"He wants to buy a truck?"

"No, sir. A special order. Soupbones. A truckload of soupbones."

"Soupbones but no truck? Are you sure that's what he said?"

"That's what he said, sir. Soupbones."

"Well, then. Sign the order and send it on."

VI

Otterby's report reached headquarters before the deadline, and after two days of waiting for another phone call that never came, he knew this time he had done his duty. He saw no more of Willy for three weeks, and gave no more thought to the truckload of soupbones than he did to the ab-sent rows of Phantoms that thundered from the runway every morning and afternoon of every day of the week.

Late one afternoon in April Otterby's assistant stuck his head into Otterby's office. "Sir, it's Willy again. He wants a word with you. He claims he's not here to ask for anything this time. Says he's here to thank you."

"I'm here to thank you, sir," said Willy as he straightened himself to attention before Otterby. Willy was not dressed in his ordinary fatigues but in parade uniform. "The men want me to thank you for going out of the way for them. We're all grateful, sir."

"I'm grateful to you and the men, Willy," said Otterby. He thought of quarterbacks interviewed after televised victories. "I couldn't do it alone.

We all work together."

"We want to show our thanks in a special way, sir, and that's why I'm here." He handed Otterby a white envelope. "We've heard rumors about your promotion sir."

Otterby suppressed an embarrassed grin and tore the back side of the envelope open. In elegant type appeared a short announcement: "Sunday Dinner in Honor of Lieutenant Colonel Frank Otterby. Full Parade Dress. Dinner served only at 1 p.m."

"Permission requested, sir, to go forward with this."

"Sure," said Otterby. "I think you should go ahead if you really feel like it."

So on the last day of April a host of men assembled early in the great messhall to make preparations for the feast of that day. Breakfast was not served. The few who found their way to the door of the hall early found it barred, with a small sign reading "No breakfast this Sunday" tacked on it. At the rear of the building a blue semi-trailer with no military markings had backed to within a foot of the loading door.

By noon a few soldiers had drifted toward the messhall. Finding the door barred they milled around smoking. At the back of the crowd stood Dorner, Robinson, and Cowgill, the three of them blind to everything but the rumors floating around.

"So that's why Lund won't come?" asked Robinson.

"That's what he said," said Dorner. "When I stopped by to see if he was coming, he just said no. He said he'd been doing some thinking, and he'd figured out it was Otterby's fault."

"That's crazy. He's just trying to keep from taking the blame himself."

"And he said that since it was Otterby's fault he wasn't going to a dinner in Otterby's honor. He said he wanted to sleep."

"Screw him, then."

"I heard someone say Lund's queer."

They were interrupted by a skinny soldier shouting from the third step of the messhall. "No food unless you're in your Sunday best. It's Otterby's orders."

At twenty minutes before the hour another word began spreading. "Get in line. No one out of line gets food. Family-style today, so find a table." The mass of men unravelled, and, as the hour of one approached, a hush fell over them.

As if by magic the door opened two minutes after the hour. No hand was seen moving it. There was no surge toward the door, for only two could have passed through at a time, and the Sunday sun and parade uniforms put everyone on their best behavior. Within twenty minutes all were seated, and as the last handful of men found empty places at the rows of tables, a quiet amazement took possession of the faces in the hall. For the messhall had been transformed. A bulbous cluster of balloons was suspended from the hall's ceiling, and from within its mass streams of red, white and blue crepe paper emanated to all parts of the hall. Across the front and back strings of American flags were hung like drapes, and even the hall's six windows had been fitted with matching paper curtains. Behind the cafeteria line, where the men usually stood their turns for a bowl of soup, a flag covering most of the hall's southern wall was hung. And before each man was a paper placemat featuring the faces of all the American presidents.

Before the hush in the hall dissipated, the kitchen door opened and the chief cook, a thin man who always had an unlit cigarette in his mouth, emerged. "Everyone please stand," he commanded. As the noise of chairs and tables diminished, the cook spoke again. "Colonel Otterby."

The room hesitated at first but then quivered with polite applause as Otterby paused in the kitchen doorway a moment before doffing his hat. As the applause grew he began walking to the head table raised on a small platform under the string of flags at the front of the hall. Behind him walked Willy, who pulled Otterby's chair and signaled for the men to sit. Then, with a nod from Willy, the kitchen door opened again.

For a moment no one emerged, even as necks craned. Then, like jets peeling off from a close formation, a line of Vietnamese girls in short red skirts fanned out into the hall, each bearing a full tray overhead. The roar that greeted them subsided only when the wolf-calls trailed off into a more persistent spattering of applause. At the head table a smile of approval spread on Otterby's face, and Willy took the place next to him.

"You'd think the war was over," said Robinson across the table to Dorner in one of the corners of the hall.

"You sound like Lund now," complained Cowgill.

"I wonder where Otterby got all those whores to wait on tables," said Robinson. "He must have trucked them up from Saigon."

"Or raided a village."

"And taken only teenage virgins," said Dorner.

"There's no such thing as a yellow virgin. Those whores are born in sin. Ask Lund. He knows, and that's why he won't dare show his face on Sundays."

"If he came to this table right now I wouldn't move over for him. You saw the way he treated us. He took that dog away like it was an empty sack of flour. He just turned his back on us like it was all *our* fault."

"So let him keep to himself from now on."

"There was something big I had to face in those days, Willy, and that's why I closed myself in," continued Otterby. "I had to explain what happened to the village outside Nha Trang, the one that got hit."

"By mistake, sir?"

"Yes, by mistake. I tried to explain it up the line, but I had a problem. And then I thought it through. These things are mechanical and human."

"Sir?"

"The computer, Willy. There was an error made."

"So you told them, sir?"

"No, I didn't blame the computer. I didn't mention that. It was Norman's fault. You remember Norman?"

"Norman, sir?"

"The young spotter who bailed out over the jungle. The one they found hanging in a tree."

"Jesus Christ! I remember now."

"He's dead now, poor boy, but it was his fault. That's what I told them, and they agreed. And maybe Norman got what he deserved. There were a lot of people killed in that village."

"And Lund's only getting what he deserves," said Dorner. "He thinks he's smarter than us."

"He's got a *de*-gree."

"So he can go screw himself from now on."

"I can see, Willy, that you know this war's no picnic. I remember Korea. They used to give us medals then. It didn't used to be this way. Now I've got to wait for orders to shoot the old German Shepards we had locked up in back."

"Goddamn, I can't believe my eyes," said Robinson. "Those whores are bringing us lamb. We're all getting a leg of lamb."

"What's that those whores are bringing out, Willy?" asked Otterby.

"It's an Italian dish. *Agnellino con salsa d'alici*. My mother used to make it."

"What the hell is that?"

"Legs of lamb, sir."

Otterby gave him a sideways glance.

"They got in, sir. The people we closed the deal with got them in for us. It was part of the deal. But we got something special for you, sir."

Four of the red-skirted girls danced toward the table, each of them holding an edge of a big silver tray. They stopped before Otterby, curtsied together, and slid the tray on the table before him.

"For you, sir, the whole thing," said Willy. "We used to do it this way every Easter Sunday. We used to eat the head too, sir, but I told them to save it for us. It's the best part."

"You're spoiling me, Willy. How can I turn you down after a banquet like this? I just don't see how you do it."

"I guess you could say I'm able to respond, sir."

"But what's this whole show costing us?"

"Sir, we don't talk business on Sundays."

"No, I suppose not," Colonel Otterby said as he leaned back in his chair. "Best let sleeping dogs lie."

19

THE MASK

Colonel Frank Otterby let out a long and weary breath.

"So that's the story I'm letting you in on. You know there's only two ways you can go wrong—human or mechanical. There are two factors— men and machines—and they can go wrong. Somehow or other a plane went wrong and a village was bombed. People are sad, but they know this is war and these things happen. I'd like to say I'm sorry, but how can you say you're sorry?"

His eyes drifted to the white wall behind the four men seated in front of him. All five men in the room averted their eyes from the mask made of bamboo sticks that sat like a strange birdcage before them on Otterby's desk.

"My problem is simple. I could explain everthing in a report. There are two ways you can go wrong. My problem is morale. It's a hard thing to ask, because I know how you feel. But we've got to think about the men. We don't want them fretting and talking, because then they get jumpy and we've got another mistake. So I don't want you to spread around what you saw out there. When they ask you what happened to Norman, you tell them he was shot down and you found him and that's all."

Norman had been missing for days on a reconnaissance mission. They even stopped looking for him. They found him only because they smelled him. The four of them walked within ten feet and would have missed him had a breeze from the tree on which he was hanging not stirred itself and called them back.

Even then they did not know who it was. He was suspended like a bloated scarecrow some fifteen feet up in the tree, his head not visible from the ground. Andy, who normally volunteered for nothing, climbed the tree and cut the parachute straps that had tangled themselves in some of the upper branches. Thus it was Andy who first saw a thing so horrible that when he came down from the tree his face was as blanched as a bone. "Oh God, Oh God," was all he said.

When Lund, one of the others on the patrol, saw what Andy had seen, he pulled out a pistol, and almost before Andy could scramble out of the way Lund began firing at the corpse crumbled at the base of the tree. "Dirty gooks!" he screamed as he fired three bursts at the body. He stopped firing only because one of the others grabbed his arm.

They did not know it was Norman until they got back to the base with the body and examined the dogtags. That's when they found out his real name was Norman. Everyone thought his name was Butch, the name he brought with him to the base. And Andy, the skinny twenty-year-old who carried a light but big-boned strength on his six-foot frame and who once made himself so scarce that he grew hair that showed even when he had his helmet on, was "The Girl," even after Otterby, when he saw it, made him shave his head to the skin.

Norman came from Warren, a suburb on the northwest side of Detroit that kept spreading because the housing developers promised no-money-down deals and safety for white women and their daughters. The people were mostly newcomers to the area, coming to work in the new one-story windowless brick factories from farms that were failures, from grocery stores and gas stations that had gone out of business in small towns away from the new superhighways, and from shacks in the hills of Kentucky, Tennessee and southern Ohio. Norman's father came from a Jackson, Ohio chicken farm to a job in an auto parts plant during World War II. Within a year he had bought a small squat house with two bedrooms and no basement for two hundred dollars down. Norman was the second of the blond-headed brothers born two years apart to the stout woman with short legs and big breasts whom his father met one Friday night in a cozy corner bar and made pregnant two weeks later in the front seat of his Ford. This woman had photographs taken of the boys on their second birthdays. She had the pictures framed and hung on the living room wall, where both of them with the eager blue eyes and blond faces of salesmen smiled out at visitors in the home.

Norman was a few inches shorter than most of his friends, but he was broad-chested and big in the shoulders. He wore his hair in a flat crewcut and grinned horizontally when someone spoke to him. His older brother bullied him until he was too old to live at home. After his brother left, Norman felt that he had all the freedom he would ever need in the small bedroom in which he had spent most of his life pushed into a corner, touched by the shadows of his father and mother only when they accused him of sin with their looks.

By the time he was fifteen Norman decided to transform himself. He spent the summer performing outrages with booze and cars sure to catch the attention of girls in general, not one of whom he dared ask out on a date. By the end of the summer, he had shed the soft skin he spent ten years growing around himself in the corner of his small bedroom. And although his crowd thought him a bit crazy, they counted him in more often than not.

21

It was the times he was not counted in that made him shrink. "When are you going to grow up?" his father yelled at him one September night. "Why don't you quit hanging around and do something with your life?"

The next morning Norman found himself in the football coach's office. "So you want to come out for the team?" The coach was sunk in a chair, leering up at him out of a shadow cast over his eyes by a baseball cap. "What makes you think you can come out two weeks late?"

Norman stood in silence with his hands in his pockets, his wide grin steadier than his legs.

"And what makes you think you can do anything for us?"

"From the sound of things, sir. Yesterday I heard some people talking about this year's team and I watched practice from outside the fence, and I liked the way it sounded."

The coach's eyes seemed to cross in confusion for a moment, but he took the answer at face value. "It's tough, you know. Football's tough. What position do you play?"

"Quarterback or halfback."

"What's your name, son?"

"Norman."

That afternoon the coach took one look at him and sent him to a group of seven trying to make the junior varsity as linemen. For the next three weeks he took his position with the others, closing his eyes just before the big seniors rammed into the dummy he held. He made the varsity as a substitute, and after long periods of pacing back and forth along the sidelines like a caged animal, he finally got into one game long enough to recover a fumble that led to a touchdown in one of the team's three victories of the year. In the glare of that moment the only thing that stuck was his new name. He remembered that the coach, delirious with the fever of victory and unable to remember his name, thumped him on the helmet with his fist and called him "Butch," a name that became his until the end of his days.

After that Norman was half-sure that the girls whispered as he passed, and it was this dim faith that made him try again the following fall. He was bigger now and faster, so he told his coach he wanted to be a fullback. His team lost its first three games with him at fullback, but Norman saw his dreams come true every time he broke from the huddle and took his place on the field.

Norman's dreams were cut short by two words. "A girl," the coach called him, "A girl." The coach threw the words at Norman a second time as he paused during a halftime of silent pacing to single Norman out and dash the words against his face. And Norman believed the coach. He was a girl because he tried to skirt around a tackler instead of lowering his head and bulling straight ahead. The coach whacked him on the helmet as he ran out for the second half. "Run over them," he screamed at Norman, who sprinted onto the field weak from the mad beating of his own heart.

He tried running over them the rest of the year, and he closed his eyes. Every time the team broke from the huddle he took his position, feeling the weight of the helmet on his head and glaring ahead through the two iron bars protecting his face at the red eyes of the linemen waiting for him. He took the ball with his head already down and ordered his legs to go. When his head met the inevitable wall, his legs collapsed first, and then his body caved in under him like an empty sack dropped to the ground.

In the back rows of the grandstand the boys who stole swallows of wine from bottles hidden in paper bags howled every time he went down. Before the season was over he was back on the sidelines pacing, more slowly now as the weight of his shame pressed down on him. "Keep your helmet on," the coach yelled at him one time when he dared to show his face. "I want everyone on the bench to keep his helmet on. And sit down with the rest. Your pacing is driving me crazy." By the time he gathered the courage to look back at the crowd one more time, he knew that even the cheerleaders were laughing at him.

But he never heard them laugh, even when the boys he drank beer with in parked cars asked him if he would turn into a war protestor like some of the girls on the student council. "Hell no," he said. "I'd rather be dead than red."

II

It was more than nine months after Norman received his induction notice that his body was found in the tree and carried down the hill. He had flown sixty-seven missions. He had listened carefully to the instructors who schooled him at the base, and he had underlined notes explaining the steps he was to follow from the time he started his engine to the time he felt his wheels touch down. "Take two readings of every suspected target," the instructor told him. "And don't just fly over once. You have to slant in to see what's really going on."

On all his missions he looked for suspicious activity as he swept over and across the fields and treetops, and whenever he saw a group of villagers run for cover as he flew in close for a second look he marked the coordinates on his charts. More than once he had to prod himself back to attention as the beautiful landscape below rolled on and on until it met the liquid blue sky, caught him in its tranquil drift and carried him beyond the charts and the instrument panel and the frail wings of the plane blowing like a paper kite in the wind.

But he always returned with at least a new target marked on his charts. One day Otterby called him to his office and pinned a medal on his chest. Norman carried the medal in his pocket everywhere he went.

It did not bother him that some of the targets he marked on his charts were trees and fields. He handed his charts to a skinny officer with glasses who said nothing and threw them on a desk.

"Because they don't give a goddamn," a soldier who worked in the office whispered to him one night. "They just want the forms filled out so they can sit on their asses and send paper work back and forth to each other."

"Bullshit," Norman said weakly.

"So they can keep themselves busy. You've never seen *them* in the bush, have you?"

"So you think the charts just end up on somebody's desk?"

"That's right. That skinny bastard with the goggles just throws all those papers on his desk and shuffles them like a pack of cards. Then he plays solitaire with them every night until he gets too drunk to stay awake any more."

"I don't believe you," said Norman, "because I've seen the holes the bombers have left in the ground."

"Because they're just dropping their load. They just go out there in the middle of nowhere and drop their load. It's like screwing. Sometimes you just close your eyes and pound away. You don't care if she's ugly or what. You just pound away."

III

"And it's a fucking shame," Otterby kept telling the four soldiers in his office who had found Norman's body. "I'm very sorry we lost that boy."

He stood, pointing at the bamboo mask on his desk. "And this. I don't understand it. Why did they have to put this cage over his head? Wasn't it enough to shoot him down? What kind of animals would think of something like that cage? I was in the World War and I never saw anything like this. There you knew the enemy and you didn't have politicians tying one hand behind your back. I was in Korea and there you fought for every inch of ground until you owned it. And there were some tragic things, but not like this. They're like rats, these people. They hide in holes like rats and they eat like rats. Sometimes I want to take bulldozers out there in the bush and just start burying them in their holes."

He turned toward them and required the four to look up at him. "Because we've got good men I don't want to lose," he continued. "Because they know right from wrong. So like I said before, I don't want the others talking. When they ask you about Butch, you forget about the mask. You tell him he was shot down and you found him and that's all."

He extended a hand that asked each of them to seal their gentleman's agreement.

Otterby knew only half the horror. Only the four who found Norman knew the whole secret behind the mask. And only Andy had stared the horror, and Norman, in the face.

There were two incidents. One developed during a game of touch football, a ragtag affair organized on a Saturday afternoon outside the messhall. "So we can work up a good beer-drinking thirst," said one of the privates who always won big at the late Saturday night poker games. "And so Butch can prove he was a high school hero."

They all laughed except Norman, who when he was given the ball ran until he saw someone about to tag him and then ducked his head down and tried to ram his way.

"It's like executing someone with a howitzer," one of the soldiers complained. "That jerk doesn't understand that touch football is like tennis, not football."

"He told me it's instinct," said another who had been rammed. "But if someone's going to get hurt it won't be me next time."

"He used to be a fullback, the kind of machine you shift into drive and crash into walls."

"The fucker told me he went to a place called Troy High. He said everyone called him the human Trojan."

"Because his legs are made of rubber."

"No, because all the ugly girls would use him once and throw him away."

"No, because he always got his head busted whenever he tried screwing it into anything."

"I'm going to screw a fist into his face the next time he rams me."

They all had things to say except Andy, who lined up across from Norman each time the ball was centered and saw Norman's red eyes sunk behind taut jawbones, the eyes glaring not at but beyond him and beyond the blue evening sky on the horizon just beginning to show a haze the color of anger. And it was Andy who best managed to avoid Norman's mad bursts by gliding to one side like a cat every time Norman came near.

"Way to go, 'Girl,' " the players on Andy's team said as he brought Norman's rushes to a soft stop. The words ate their way into Norman's brain where, once the action stopped, they burned.

Nothing would have come of the matter had Otterby not appeared to cheer the game with an approving smile, for when Norman saw Otterby out of the corner of his eye his heart made a long pause and his words came between convulsed breaths.

"Give me the ball," he said. "I'm going to bury that fag this time."

A smile curled on Norman's face as he took his place. When he received the ball he took five steps to his right, stopped, and reversed his field.

Andy, his arms outspread and his face wry and ready, waited.

The moment of impact occurred a long second later than Norman expected. When Norman opened his eyes he found himself flying, the sky turning in bewilderment around him as he, suspended, reached for something to grasp. There there was a jolt and he saw Andy standing over him, a smile wide on his face.

"You fucking fag," Norman cried while still on the ground. "I saw you sucking cocks behind the messhall." Then he picked himself up, found the football he had dropped, and threw it point-blank at Andy, who turned just in time to take it in the small of the back. "A fag," Norman screamed as he walked away, "a long-haired fucking fag!"

Everyone waited. They knew more would come of it, even though Andy seemed too indifferent to do anything more than sit and smoke opium under an elm tree behind the messhall with an old Vietnamese rag-picker who somehow made his way into camp every night. Norman's chance came at a poker game the following night. Neither was playing but both had gathered to watch a group of six play their final hands. Norman started the trouble:

"If you were the Girl you'd have four queens to play," Norman said to one of the six.

"Get screwed," someone said.

"I got screwed better than anyone here," Norman said. "Just before I shipped out here. A thirty-eight year-old. Divorced. I screwed her all night—you know, like Dustin Hoffman. That old bitch was my Mrs. Robinson."

Everyone laughed except Andy. "No, you didn't feel like Dustin Hoffman," Andy said.

"What the fuck do you know?"

"Dustin Hoffman felt bad. That's what I know."

Norman flew over the poker table at Andy before anyone could stop him, his fists flailing wildly.

"This guy's nuts," someone laughed.

"He's drunk."

"I don't think so. He's crazy, that's what he is. He needs locking up."

So they locked him up for the night.

"In one of those cages," someone told Andy. "The ones they use for tigers. He's madder than hell, so you'd better watch out. They can keep him locked up in there for a while, but someday he's gonna be out."

Weeks later Lund tried to talk to Andy after rumors about Norman's death began spreading and after the old rag-picker Andy used to smoke opium with had been shot trying to get into the base through a hole in the fence.

"So now we know how the old man got in and out every night, and it's amazing he didn't get it sooner. But we still don't know about Butch."

"The guy was screwed up," Andy said.

"But why? Why the cage around his head? Why put the cage around his head? There's something you saw."

"What I see is my own business and nobody else's. Therefore I saw nothing."

"But the mask? The cage they put over his head?"

Andy had nothing to say.

"But the mask didn't kill him, did it? I hear it was just fit over his head with plenty of room to spare."

"No. I don't know."

"They just locked that thing over his head and left him there to die?"

Andy did not agree.

"So you make nothing of it?"

"Nothing."

"Nothing?"

"How am I supposed to know? I'm not in intelligence. I'm a draftee. Ask Otterby."

But not even Otterby had seen what the four others saw after Andy cut Norman down from the tree—not what was left of Norman's face, or the rat, huddled in the back corner of the mask, leering with red eyes, fat around the neck, and smug like a sleeping cat.

V

It was Otterby's smile that stayed with Norman on his last flight. For as the landscape flowed by beneath him, he saw Otterby's smile confirming what he remembered his father had said, the father who loomed in the house like a giant shadow a few hours each evening, and who spoke, when he did at all, in the imperative.

Norman remembered a vague day, many years ago, when he had come to his father in tears. He knew that his father would say little. "What are you crying about?" he shouted. "Are you a sissy?"

"No," he said weakly, wiping his eyes with his sleeve. His mother was a sissy because he had heard her cry at night. Then he told his father all about it—how his brother had taken it from him, stolen it right out of his hands, and how his brother pushed him in the face when he tried to take it back.

His father listened for once. He saw his father's eyes looking at the wall behind him, as if in that space was written a long outrageous past. And he saw his father's face turn red the way it did when he yelled at his mother.

"Now you see here, boy," his father shouted as he grabbed Norman's arm. "I want my boys to know right from wrong, and I want them to stand up for their rights. Now you tell him it's yours, and don't you let him push you around. You take it back from him, and you tell him I said so. And if he pushes you, you push him back. If you push long and hard, you'll win— and if you don't, you leave it up to me."

"I'll show him," Norman told himself as he went in search of his brother. His eyes already were narrow when he burst into the bedroom. "Give it to me! Give it to me!" he screamed, and he kept screaming as he began flailing away blindly with both fists. Finally his brother, holding him off with one arm, took a small rubber ball out of his pocket and, with a sassy laugh, threw it at him before ducking out of the room.

Norman remembered that his brother laughed about the incident at the special dinner the family had for Norman the day he was to leave for boot camp. Norman did not think it was funny then, but he kept the peace. When, on his last flight, the incident renewed itself in his mind, he again was quiet, the vague glare of his humiliation droning away with the engines of the plane that carried him away.

When the huddle of huts suddenly appeared beneath him he was more confused than surprised. He glanced at his charts to see if a village showed on them, but he drew a blank. Without banking in for a look he put the plane in a steep dive until he was sure he saw people moving about. Then he pulled out of his dive, marking the coordinates on his target chart as he left the village behind.

A half-hour later he heard the engine sputter and saw black smoke coming from it. He glanced at the instrument panel and saw needles dancing wildly. His voice was steady when he signaled his mayday over the radio. "Mechanical failure," he said. "I'll have to bail out." Before he could give a reading of his position he felt a soft thump jolt the plane's left wing and he saw a piece of the wing tear away and disappear into the wind behind him. "They're shooting at me!" he cried into his radio, the realization coming to him more slowly than the words. The plane seemed to arch its back for one last salute in the sky before he found himself fumbling for the latch to the cockpit door. When his hand touched the cold metal a paralysis went through him. The engine had died and the plane, suddenly silent, had begun falling like a stone. He held fiercely to the latch while the sky began circling wildly.

Suddenly there was another jolt and he felt himself being carried away in a sharp blast of cold wind. It took him a moment to realize he had been thrown free, but that moment he found the ripcord and pulled at it. He saw nothing beneath him as he felt the lines and silk unravelling, but when the hard tug came assuring him that the chute had opened, his senses righted themselves and he saw himself floating down instead of toward the center of an empty blue sky.

The dark green of the landscape below came into view. He drew in a deep breath. Except for the wind boiling inside the umbrella of his parachute, it was quiet. He relaxed his grip on the main lines. To his left he saw a level green field. He would come down there, he thought, in a clearing where he could easily be seen from a chopper, especially if he spread his chute on the grass. Otterby would come for him in a minute or two, and his father would be with him.

Then as he looked down a nausea rose from his stomach. To the left of the field he saw a thicket of brush and bamboo, and beyond it another field. He would float free, clear the thicket and come down in the distant field. As a dizziness worked itself like a wave through his body, he thought of the way Andy walked. Andy never seemed to touch the ground when he walked or when he used to spring out at him like a cat. He felt no anger now. "I should have just gotten up without saying a word and walked to my side of the field," he thought. "That would have been the right thing to do." He closed his eyes and released his hold on the straps, and with his eyes closed he saw the wind making waves over the field and felt himself descending softly into a bed of grass.

He floated down hanging from the chute with his arms outstretched before a gust of wind brought him back to consciousness. When he opened his eyes he saw he was less than a hundred feet from the ground, swept past the field over a forest spotted with leafless trees and bamboo. "Oh God," he cried, "Oh God!"

The small men who had emerged from their tunnels below did not hear his words or see the change that came over his face. They simply stood with their weapons lowered, waiting for the wind to finish its work before they began to work their justice on one more intruder from the sky.

THE GIRL AND TWO OLD MEN

When Andy dared to open his eyes, he still did not know where he was. "What am I doing in the grass?" he asked himself. "How did I end up where I am?"

The pain that seared into his chest no longer burned. In the silence he felt nothing but the numbness of his legs and the shiver that passed through him after his hand discovered the blood covering his shirt. "They got the old man," he thought, "and now they got me."

When he closed his eyes parts of the dream reappeared. The day was blue, the grass undulating like waves in the wind, and there, just ahead, was a beach where girls tossed long hair over their heads in rhythm with the washing of the sea. And further out, miles beyond a red buoy bobbing like a bottle cork, he saw Uncle Victor floating on his back.

Then a small man in black suddenly stood straight up in the grass to his left. For a moment he thought the man was waving at him, and he paused to look again to be sure. Someone shouted. Then from behind something so hot and terrible tore into him that he collapsed like a rag dropped to the ground.

When he lifted his head again he was hidden by the shadows of the grass. The sun, veiled by a yellow haze, slanted in on him, silent but aware of his hiding place. He felt a dull fatigue in his arms and a brittle numbness in his chest. If he tried to lift himself everything would crumble and cave in like old plaster. So nothing mattered except the breeze gliding over the grass above his face and the beat of his own heart straining like a man running through a city street.

He wanted to sleep. He had grown tired of following the man in front of him, tired of the daily patrols that led nowhere in search of an enemy he never saw. He was tired of Otterby screaming at everyone. They'll blow your brains out when you're not looking. You go out all day looking for them and you never find them. You can't get them into lines—can't get them to face you right on, and you can't sit with your backs toward the inside of a circle, because then they never show themselves. You can't make a ring around them and put the squeeze on, because they always slip

30

out of it. There's no logic in their heads, no plain sense. But when you're not looking there they are, and they'll kill you sure as shit. And you can't trust any of them. They could be anyone—a boy too young to be fucked, or some old man too old to do anything but kill you when you're looking the other way.

No, no, Andy thought. They couldn't be anyone. Not the old ragpicker. He couldn't be one of them.

Otterby said they came back to kill anyone left behind. So he had to run into the trees to hide until someone came to take him home. He felt the urge to sprint just as he had sprinted that day in the water—not toward the buoy or the shore but wildly into a Pacific heaving waves so high they felt like walls collapsing in on him. He tried reaching for his Uncle Victor's arms, those sagging arms that once had saved him, passing their strength into him until the old man knew the boy was able to walk the last fifty feet to shore by himself. And now his arms felt as they did that day in the Pacific when he lost sight of Uncle Victor, the buoy, and the shore. He was too tired to lift his arms. He wouldn't be able to make it to the trees.

So he would hide in the grass until the others came, and maybe the regular old ragpicker would come with them. The ragpicker smoked opium with him under the elm behind the messhall, the two of them facing not the rows of trash barrels but the fence marking out the base's eastern perimeter and beyond that the fields and sky that faded from yellow into gray and eventually blackness as evening slowly fell.

But then he gave up even the hope that the old ragpicker would come, because he remembered that they had killed him—that after he heard the three bursts of gunfire and ran toward the hole in the fence, all the time saying to himself, "Oh God, no. No. Not the old ragpicker. Oh God, no," he saw him lying in a heap just inside the fence, his white shirt shining in the glare of the spotlight that zeroed him against the black of night.

Since that night he kept looking for the old ragpicker, kept waiting out of habit for his return, even though he knew he would never come back. Once, in Saigon, he saw an old man duck inside a doorway, but by the time he forced himself through the crowd he found the doorway empty and dark and he was afraid to go in. And one afternoon, along National Highway 14, his column passed an old man, a cart, and a mule. As they approached each other their eyes, suddenly free of confusion and fear, met for one still moment, but before he could gesture or speak the man took the mule by the ear and turned away toward the grass alongside the road.

A chill passed like a wave through him. He knew he was sinking when he saw the old ragpicker's face converge with Uncle Victor's, both faces turning together slowly at first, swirling away from him, dissolving into the gray sky into which he was sinking. Before he closed his eyes he saw them clearly again—the old ragpicker sitting like a Buddha under the elm tree, and his Uncle, his arms stretched out lazily at his sides, floating like a raft on the Pacific, the faces of the two old men touching and floating away from him. This he saw when he made one more effort to pull his knees up under his chin, when he knew that, although he could not move his arms or legs, he had not yet drowned. He knew this because he knew that when a man drowns his life flashes before him just before he goes down for the final time.

II

They were decent enough, but he avoided them all: his parents, his football coach, the students at the beach, the soldiers who told him never to volunteer, the strangers who sooner or later appeared on crowded side-walks, even in Columbus, his home town. When he arrived in Vietnam he lay in his bunk silently hating them, never raising his voice to complain. He knew only that he wanted to get away. Others tried to get him drunk so they could laugh while they jabbed at the secrets behind his eyes. But he knew of no secrets inside himself. So when they came to ask him to drink, he always said no. They talked fast and easy, had jokes and stories to tell. He could not laugh, and he had no story to tell.

Maybe the reason he liked to sit and smoke opium with the old rag-picker was that with him he could forget about the short and disconnected explanations his parents gave him—pieces of string rolled into a ball, the ends lost in the middle. The old man used to come into the compound each night through a hole in fence, nosing around the barracks and messhall, picking things out of trash barrels and putting them into a brown bag he carried over his back. He came mainly for rags, he said. Everyone got so used to him they thought he was a regular kitchen hand, and even the soldiers who knew he came and went every night through the hole in the fence paid no attention to him. He was at least ninety years old, his face sagging under the weight of wide wrinkles that reminded him of the thick hide of an old tree. Lund once told Andy he feared for the old man—he expected him to be blown to bits some night because the perimeter was full of mines. And Andy, who used to watch the old man disappear into the field behind the messhall each night after they had had their smoke, tried to warn him by drawing in the dirt. The old man smiled at the boy, pointing to his head and then his nose. "Snake," he said, "I snake,"—and he made a wavy motion with his hand as if he were slithering through grass.

He came and went. The first time the old man, gleaming at him with a gold tooth, showed him the pipe and opium behind the messhall, Andy smoked with him. That evening the two of them sat down under the elm for the first time and silently passed the old man's pipe. They sat a full hour under the tree, listening to the lizards that sometimes stirred, staring vacantly at the hills slowly fading into the shadow of night. The old man came back the next night and they passed the pipe again, the old man sitting with his legs crossed beneath him until, as if responding to a signal given by a lizard in the night, he struggled to his feet, threw the bag over his back, and limped into the dark.

Andy waited for him every night after that. At first they tried to speak through words and gestures. The ragpicker's wife was dead and he had lost two sons in the wars. One daughter had gone away with the French and he had not seen another for ten years. The wars, he said, are bad, and he drew an "X" on the ground. "I—no fight," he said, pointing to his eyes. "Old—old," he said. By the second week they seldom spoke. Instead they smoked in silence and watched the evening fade until the old man rose and limped into the dark.

Andy felt good after smoking the opium. When he was in his bunk the darkness revolved in slow circles, drawing him away from thoughts about what he was doing in this strange place where days seemed yellowed by a haze hovering over the fields, and where his only companions were crude boys older than the ones abandoned when he left the yellow smell of his high school locker room for the last time without telling his coach he quit.

On the nights the old man failed to show, Andy wandered over the grounds until night fell, then returned to the barracks and watched the men play cards. On these nights he seldom slept. He could not be like these men. They started calling him "The Girl" after Otterby saw him with his hair grown down over his ears and made him shave his head. He knew they were thinking he was queer even after he showed them he was the best player in the football games they played on Saturdays.

He played the games because they would not leave him alone. He played, that is, until one Saturday evening a soldier they all called Butch tried to pick a fight with him, and he, trying to protect himself from Butch's mad rushes, cut him down. He did not want to hurt Butch and tried to break his fall, but Butch, before walking off the field, picked up the football and hit him in the small of the back with it.

That was the last time he saw Butch alive. He was the one who, a few days later, found Butch dead, tangled in a tree with a cage, a booby-trap, attached to his head. He climbed the tree and cut him down, but saw something so horrible in the cage that for a week he did not talk. He did not know it was Butch until Otterby called him in to warn him not to tell others what he had seen. Because, he said, it would ruin morale.

So he kept quiet, just as he said nothing when he walked out on the coach. Whenever the coach turned his back during practice sessions, Andy stole glances from the girls in short skirts walking by, or he daydreamed while looking at the changing colors of the trees that shimmered in the sun. Then he let his hair grow long. Two weeks later the coach told him his hair was bad for the team, and the next Monday morning he waited until the coach went on his coffee break before sliding the note under his door on which he had scrawled the words, "I don't want to play any more. I quit. Andy."

"What do you mean, you quit," his coach hissed at him after pulling him out of a study hall that afternoon. "It's just that you look like a damned girl out there. I said to myself, I've got to help this boy, there's something bothering him. So you can't quit on me now. I'm counting on you—everyone is counting on you." The hallway was empty except for a janitor leaning on his broomhandle. The coach stuffed two one-dollar bills in Andy's shirt pocket. "For a haircut," he said. "Think it over. And keep the money no matter what you decide."

He spent that afternoon in the park sitting under a tree and looking up through the branches at the sky and the clouds. As a chill breeze came up he found himself wandering home to the face of his father, who looked up from a plateful of chicken bones. "They called me today from school," he said. "They told me all about it. Sit down, son, and eat."

He did not eat. He sat looking at his plate and his mother turned away from him. "They told me they wanted you to turn out right. They took films of you and they had scouting reports. When you were only a sophomore you proved them right. Now they don't know anymore. Your hair has to go, and your mother will give you the money."

He scored on a long touchdown run the following Friday night. It was easier this way, he thought. As the blue skies of October faded before the damp November days, he resumed the routine, and after the last game was played he and five others parked in a field and got drunk.

When spring finally came he felt the old urge and he let his hair grow long again. Then he and his only close friend, an intelligent but shy and skinny boy named David, drove to the university district and sat in the booth of a hamburger joint watching the faces parading before them on the sidewalks. Andy said little to David during the hours they sat watching. They broke the silences by putting dimes in the juke-box at their booth.

One night Andy turned his head toward the window and saw a short dark man with black eyes looking in at him. The man stood at the window a moment, and, as if satisfied that Andy had seen him, broke into a grin. Andy quickly turned away as if he had seen nothing, and when he looked again the man was gone.

They left later than usual that night, but as he walked alongside the traffic lining the street he noticed that the sky was filled with wires crossing above the streets like a net made of steel filaments. He followed some of the wires with his eyes, but they disappeared into the dark. Somehow it all seems to work, he thought. The cars stop on red and go on green. Someday, he told himself, he would see it all from above—from there he would be able to see if the wires, traffic and people formed some sort of jumbled pattern like the one he had seen in an abstract painting once.

He did not see the dark man again for two months. He and David by then were confident that with their new long hair their high school faces would draw no stares. One night Andy saw the dark man on the street talking to people passing by. By the time he and David were close enough to see the man's face they saw him suddenly stumble forward, pushed from behind by a squat youth in a sweatshirt. "Watch where you're going. You're blocking traffic," the youth shouted at him. The dark man put up a hand to protect himself from the blond face jeering at him, but the youth pushed it away, punched him in the stomach, and, as the dark man sank down, kicked him in the legs. "How's that, you goddam queer," he shouted, looking backward as he was jostled down the sidewalk by two of his friends.

While people looked down at the fallen man as if he had done something wrong, Andy leaned toward him until David tugged at his sleeve. When they were halfway down the block Andy looked back, but he saw nothing but the flow of people on the sidewalk. "Fuck it," he said to himself.

Neither he nor David said a word about the dark man. They talked about their plans to meet the following June at an old cabin on the ocean near San Francisco. Andy's parents received his announcement with silence, and a silence hardened on Andy's face as he began bracing himself for the final debate he knew would take place following his graduation from high school. When that fall he, without telling his coach, quit playing football before the season was three games old, his father guessed there was trouble ahead.

Andy had little to do but wait. He watched television and spent hours alone in his bedroom, a square room with a low ceiling he could almost touch as he lay on his bed. He listened to albums until he got lost between the pulses of the music and fell asleep, drowned in the music's heavy beats and in the long loud spaces lacking melody, spaces weighed down by the rhythms that kept him from floating out of bounds or out of touch with anything beyond the beating of his own heart. His mother did not understand why the music had to be played so loud, and agreed to compromise. They would pay for earphones if he would use them. He smirked like a cat when for the first time he covered his ears with the earphones and lay back in his bed, closed his eyes, and floated away into the inchoate spaces between the pulsing of the drums.

Andy paid for his earphones when he told his parents he had not changed his mind about California. "We'll see," they said. "We'll see."

The day to decide the issue arrived and he lost. A deal, they said. No, he would not stay in the cabin near San Francisco. He would go to Santa Barbara and stay with Uncle Victor, and if he agreed to enroll at the university the coming fall and live at home, they would pay his trainfare to California and his tuition when he returned.

He sealed the deal by staying at the dinner table that night rather than storming away as he had done the first time they said no, and then he went upstairs to his room and to the earphones which closed out a fading June sky. For a long hour he sat on the bed cupping his hands around his earphoned head. As he realized that he had given in without a fight, he took the earphones off and set them on the table next to the bed, where they jeered at him in a hysterical whisper. He sank into his pillow and began falling away—not into sleep but into a fatigue deeper than his boredom and defeat. He closed his eyes and felt the room circle, his body suspended yet sinking into a thick gloom until he heard footsteps echoing like metal down a narrow corridor—because he could see the sky, blue and empty, above him. I've been here before, he thought. This is the boiler room of the high school, where all the big machines and pipes and furnaces are kept. He saw them, the gray shapes curling like metallic dragons sending out tentacles into the ceiling above. It is here, he thought, that the final connection is made— here that the wires are attached. The furnace was wearing an iron mask, and between the bars he saw coals burning like angry eyes. Next to the furnace he saw the chief engineer. He had seen him before in the halls of the school, a little man who smiled and nodded like a servant when he passed. But as he came nearer he faced not the engineer but the dark man he had seen on the sidewalks. For the first time he looked deeply into the man's yellowed face. "Don't give in," the man whispered. "Don't let them make this happen to you."

The next morning the house was filled with the aroma of fresh coffee and frying bacon. It was chilly in the room so he pulled the blanket over his head, but not before he saw that it was another blue day. He lay in bed for ten minutes feeling warm. Then he made his way to the kitchen downstairs.

"Good morning, mother," he said.

"Good morning, son. I hope you slept well. I've made you your favorite breakfast." She smiled at him with soft kind eyes.

IV

When Andy finally leaned back in his seat to watch the sunset, he imagined that this is how it would feel floating in the Pacific. The train moved slowly through the cornfields of Ohio and Indiana, and as it made its constipated passage past the warehouses and slum-yards of Chicago and finally emerged into new cornfields, a wave of excitement passed through him. He seemed freer now, as if he had left all cities behind. The train seemed to glide, sliding along the silvery rails with a sleek flow interrupted only by the slight rhythmic jolt of the crossties. Like the music, he thought, but more smooth and easy-going. He turned toward the window and looked out, the poles along the tracks rushing by his face and the silver threads they carried shimmering in the dying sunlight. The horizon passed slowly to the rear, more slowly, it seemed, than the sun went down.

As the train neared California, even the air seemed free and fresh. He watched the mountains and rocks for hours, and counted the steel structures that had replaced the wood telephone poles as if they were giant robots lumbering in lines across the land.

As the train came to a halt in the station at Santa Barbara, Andy recognized his Uncle Victor, the old man standing at the side of the tracks with his arm around an overweight woman graced by a smiling face and deep kind eyes.

"This is Aunt Kay," he announced. "She is your new aunt while you stay with us."

Uncle Victor was almost eighty and the woman without a wedding ring, who he knew was not his his aunt, was thirty years younger. They shared a small square stucco house a mile from the beach. His uncle had seen the world and its wars. Two small photographs of a younger man in a uniform looked down from the living room wall. On the first day they went swimming together, Andy saw the wound too—a long gash beginning under his uncle's left rib and extending into his swim trunks. That day Andy rested on the beach exhausted from a half-hour struggle with the waves, gazing at the old man floating for a full hour on his back a hundred yards offshore, only his head visible above the water.

He wanted to float the way the old man did, but instead he learned to surf. The surfers gathered every day at noon on the beach, bringing with them loud radios. Three slender girls in bikinis teased the boys sleeping in the sun, sometimes disappearing hand-in-hand with them into the deserted dunes. Andy spent hours watching the girls, following the curves of their bodies with eyes that had hands in them, waiting for the one with dark eyes and small breasts to take him to the dunes.

But she never gave him the signal he was waiting for, and he began to resent them too. He sometimes saw the dark-eyed one looking back at him, but he turned away because he was afraid. Someday and in good time he would have the courage. Just as college happened after high school, and someday a job after college. A wife someday too, he supposed, a beautiful suntanned girl.

So every day he came to the beach with Uncle Victor, took a swim, and lay on the beach watching the old man float his hour on the sea until he emerged, his trunks hanging low enough to show his scar. Then Andy joined the group at the end of the beach, and he watched the girls in the sun until the chilly late afternoon breezes drove them away to houses Andy never saw.

It took Andy only a week to learn how to smoke grass and to discover what the others said a good high was like. It was a mellow feeling. "A buzz in the head that gave you goose pimples on the outside of the brain," one of the girls said. He laughed, even when the girl's eyes refused to focus on his.

The buzz hit him one noon after a long swim. He had been in the sun and smoked two joints, and then he felt the pulse abandon his arms and legs, his body both sinking and floating in the warm sand that seemed to draw the chill of the sea out of him, the sound of the surf humming in his head like a radio station off the air.

Every day he saw the old man's eyes watching him, and every day, sometimes nervous like a lifeguard expecting him to sink, he watched the old man float his hour at sea. When Andy returned each evening, he saw the old man lost in the day's newspapers. The three of them said little at dinner, and after dinner the old man did the dishes while Andy took his place before the television set. He usually did not hear them when they retired to bed after sitting each night watching the sun set over the thin strip of ocean visible from the back porch, and Andy was careful of noise when, sometimes after the first late movie, he lifted himself from sleep and found his bed.

And so it went. Until the last week of the summer, the week he received the letter explaining that his parents would meet his train in Chicago. It rained that week—unusual, Kay explained, for it never rained until the fall. No one appeared at the beach, but the old man went every morning to the sea, and as usual he returned an hour later. When, on the third day, the three of them sat over their morning coffee watching a light drizzle obscure the line between the sea and sky visible from the kitchen on sunny days, they all felt the gloom. Victor spoke with sharpness in his voice. "This morning you and I will swim together. We will swim out to the buoy and back." He waited before he went on. "You are too bored here in the house. There is too much boredom in you." And he tried to laugh.

So they started down the path toward the beach, Andy feeling the chill like a winter wind. He had seen the buoy bobbing above the waves, and some days, when the tide was out, it seemed close to shore. Today it disappeared behind the giant heavings of the gray ocean that seemed angry at the world.

"You are a strong swimmer?" The old man did not wait for a reply. They both knew Andy could not walk away from the ocean the old man could face alone. "She is a savage, you know, and no respecter of persons, but she will support you unless you fight her."

Andy started to wade in, just as a wave crashed against him. A wild chill went through him as his body met the cold water, and he was ready to dive into the next wave when the old man grabbed his arm.

"It's not far. You remember that," the old man shouted above the sea. "Only a hundred yards or so. But you've got to stay in control. Stay on top of her. Give yourself up to her—and do not panic. If you get tired, float the way I do. Just turn over on your back, and give yourself up to her."

He had swum three times that distance many times. Yes, it was important not to panic, to keep control. He felt his arms and legs tighten when the old man let go of his arm. "No racing," he said with a crooked smile. "Time flies when you go fast, and I'm an old man now."

And then the old man ducked his head into a wave and disappeared until Andy saw him again swimming calmly on his back at the top of a swell twenty yards to his left. As the old man sank out of view behind a higher wave, Andy felt his arms weigh him down. He tried to slow to an easy rhythm, but his legs began dragging, aching dully like his arms. He pulled up to see how much farther he had to go, but when he saw the buoy some seventy-five yards to his left, a spasm of fear went through him. He had gone off course. His legs and arms suddenly felt numb, and the pain in them was as heavy as a stone. He looked around again for the buoy just as he slid down the side of a wave. The buoy was lost. He was lost. A wave broke over his head, slapping him backward before he could catch his breath. I'm going to drown, he thought. Oh God, I'm going to drown.

The next moment he was sprinting, his hands beating wildly and his head flying from side to side. Had he not reached upward for a breath of air he would not have seen the old man some five yards ahead of him. It is too late, he thought, and he let himself go. He swallowed water and in terror fought his way to the surface. Later he remembered little except that the old man had taken hold of one arm and that when he felt the old man's hands he quit fighting, surrendered to him, just as the old man, taking him firmly by the chin, turned over on his back, lay on the waters, and slowly towed him toward shore until he was sure he could release the boy to wade the last fifty feet alone.

Half-asleep on the train back to Chicago, Andy thought about the old man and why he wanted him to swim to the buoy, and why, just before he left the small stucco house in Santa Barbara, the old man told him not to go if the government called him, not to be a fool as he, an old war dog, had been two times already, and why he loved the old man so much he never hinted to his parents that the old man was living with a woman who was neither an aunt nor a wife. But he could not make up his mind. And he did not know why he quit arguing with David about going to Canada, just as he did not know what day it was David suddenly disappeared from home, or why he himself quit college after four months and went back to handing out towels at the YWCA down the street from his house surrounded by the white fence, that same house he came to every night at ten and entered quietly to escape to the bed and music that played on in the earphones after he fell asleep.

When his draft notice came he felt relieved. It had happened to him too. More deeply than pride or fear he felt a vague assurance that he now had somewhere to go. They drove him to the train station the day he left, his father standing tall and his mother's face in tears. After he finished his training he was given three days to go home, but he lied the last time he talked to his mother on the phone and boarded the train for California instead of the eastbound plane for home, the same train from which he had once watched wide-eyed the great land pass, but in which this time he slept both day and night, not wary that the iron rails carrying him were converging to a point somewhere beyond the distant visible horizon.

V

"The round entered his back. He must have been running away," the medic said while they were lifting Andy onto the stretcher.

"I don't know what they teach them anymore. He must have got scared—just ran away. His gun's in the bushes. Not even been fired."

Andy did not hear anything until he heard the chopper's engines and felt the wild cold air beating against his face, and he did not see anything clearly until he saw arms inside the chopper reach down to lift him in. There was no fear until he saw the needle in his arm emptying itself, for again he felt the hot pain go through him, again the flesh tearing whenever he tried to move. He watched them take the needle out, then saw two faces looking down at him. Behind them he followed the lines of rivets along the metalwork of the chopper's insides, and then slowly, as he felt a giddiness in his brain, he began to see the beach and the girls and Uncle Victor floating on his back.

Someone closed a door and left him all alone. Above him two lights stared down at him. He heard the engine strain and felt his heart hover a moment before a convulsion in his stomach told him he was slanting swiftly into sky. His head felt lighter now, and he closed his eyes. Then it came back to him—that time only a few months ago when they put him with the others on the transport and when, rather than saying goodbye or thinking about where he was going across the same Pacific his Uncle Victor floated so calmly in, he saw this as a chance finally to see from above whether there was some design to the streets, some plan to the city, some tower to which all wires converged. And he was being carried away without a chance to see. All the wires disappeared before he could see, and he too faded into a haze before he could make out the shape of things below.

So maybe there was nothing to see, nothing more than the painless swell of assurance that came over him when he sat in silence with the old ragpicker under the elm.

It was black now in the boiler room, the drone of the engine a faint hum emanating from a point of light at the back of his brain. They had turned out the lights. They wanted him to sleep. You should do what you're told, they said, but never volunteer. That was good advice. Never volunteer. So he never volunteered. Now they turned out the lights and they wanted him to sleep.

So he could accept. Almost everything. Except what happened to the

40

old ragpicker. He groped in the dark trying to call him back, straining to make his eyes see the old man again. But nothing came back until he felt once more the pain rip along the left side of his chest. Then the image came into focus: the old man lying in a heap inside the fence of the camp, the spotlight shining off his white shirt.

It was this he could not accept, this that kept him from letting go. And it was this he could not forgive, not only of the two guards who stood over the old man's body impassively trying to explain, but of the others who ran up to look at him, covered him with a blanket and carried him away in a bag. He was a wild man then. They had no right to touch the old man, and he screamed until they carried him away. He fell into a bottomless sorrow after that. He never, never would volunteer.

Lund tried to talk to him. He was sorry but there was nothing they could do. These things happen, and there was nothing they could do. From that day on he never cried again, not even when he helped bring back what was left of Butch, the boy they had found hanging by his parachute straps from a tree, his head covered by a booby-trap, a cage in which he found the live rat, and not when he received the letter informing him that his Uncle had died peacefully in his bed.

He wanted to cry out to the old ragpicker but the place in his chest from where the words came had all collapsed. The old sense returned, the sense of drowning, of sinking away. It was then he saw Uncle Victor over him, reaching out with a hand. And for one instant the two old men's faces merged, as if they had known each other in some distant time. Then the faces faded and Andy knew that he would never learn to float the way his Uncle did.

The chopper suddenly lurched, and in that moment Andy's dream came to an end. "It will never be that way," he said in final bitterness just before a huge wave rose in his chest. He saw the wave hover before it began falling over him. "Fuck it," he said at last as he curled up into himself. Then, with a long farewell that said goodbye to nothing but the two old men, he quit holding his breath.

THE ENEMY

When he left his folks to get married he saw Bill, not William, printed on the birth certificate his mother delivered to him in a cigar box. On his honeymoon he and his bride saw the Hollywood musical "Showboat," and for the first time he heard the song entitled "Bill." He could remember only a phrase or two—"An ordinary guy . . . And Bill took me Upon his knee, So comfy and roomy, Feels natural to me . . ." The tune stayed with him long after his love for his bride faded and this love faded right in front of him as he watched Catherine, the preacher's wife, the soloist in his church, break into tears as she concluded her hymn. Then one day it occurred to him that the song was written for men like him, all the ordinary guys in the world.

The tune eluded him when he tried to remember it while on a mission near My Tho, the effort to bring it back as stale as the taste in his mouth and as heavy as the heat hovering over the marshes like a yellow fog. With the others he looked up to watch a Cobra slide sideways into the sky and disappear into a dot. He felt the hot air weigh him down, and he breathed it reluctantly into lungs dried by dust and cigarette smoke. No one spoke, not even when someone at the head of the column ordered everyone to quicken the pace.

Along the side of the road peasants worked in the mud, their feet lost in the riceslough and their backs bent over the earth. A stooped old man near the road looked up from his hoe as the soldiers passed, his eyes invisible behind the shadow of his hat. Bowing, he smiled just as the sun caught a golden tooth. A few of the soldiers glanced at him, and one took off his helmet and waved. The old man, still stooped, turned away and resumed his slow work with his hoe.

He had been through it before, but he might be the one hit this time. The village was just a mile ahead. The jets were coming in, and three platoons from the Second Division were to clear the southern and western roads before his squad came to the village. After the Phantoms finished their work his squad had to hold the village until an armored division passed through. Then everybody got to go home, and he, like everybody else, would return to the barracks and booze and card games that never ended but just fell apart when too many men collapsed at the table or fell into bed.

He knew there would be no enemy waiting for him. Never an enemy after the Phantoms went in. The enemy disappeared, or crawled like rats into holes no one ever found. Or the enemy walked away to some other village. He had never seen the enemy. Except when they were heaped in trucks or laid out on the ground in rows next to stacks of weapons on display for the children and old men. All of the dead, the faces, looked small. They had to be boys, but no one was sure. A soldier near the bodies once told him that anyone dead was the enemy.

Though he had been afraid before, today he was not afraid. He might get hit, but anyone might get hit. As his squad came to a ridge overlooking the village, he saw that this one was the same. A dozen or so huts made of wood, straw, scraps of metal, a clearing resembling a road wandering through. Already a few villagers moving about, ignoring the smoke and dust still rising from the pockmarks of bombs dropped only minutes ago.

Orders were given for the squad to fan out and regroup five hundred yards ahead of the clump of trees to the right of the village. Then in minutes the excitement would die. Mortar rounds would fall on the huts. Then they would follow the barrage in on foot, firing into the huts as they ran. The villagers would scatter, finding paths in the clearings between the blasts.

Only when he came down from the ridge did he feel the earth shudder, even while the last of the Phantoms faded away into its own thunder. After rushing past the thicket where the enemy was supposed to be, his heart pounded wildly as he sprayed bursts of fire into the huts he passed. His heart leaped as he saw himself among the first wave overrunning the village. But suddenly the feeling abandoned him when he realized that he had run with them to the opposite side of the village, that before him stretched a broad bare field broken only by standing water and grass. Then, as the soldiers walked back together, he came upon the villagers, some fifty in all, huddled in a group outside the central hut.

They searched the women for weapons and found one dead boy curled in a corner of one of the huts. The lieutenant ordered him placed outside the central hut. No one looked at the boy's face, no one dared touch the hand dragging backward on the ground, and no one picked up the rubber shoe that fell from his foot as he was laid outside the central hut.

And no one turned away when the dead boy's mother started a wail that cried like an ambulance returning slowly through midnight streets. He felt good when another soldier finally slapped the woman and dragged her away. The soldier ordered two older villagers to keep her quiet.

He did not know how he ended up in the hut with the other boy and the boy's grandmother. He had heard stories at the base about what happened in huts during a sweep. The men who laughed had their reasons to

43

laugh. In one village an old man stole a pair of boots after offering to clean them for nothing, and he complained when forced to bring them back. And in the bars the whores, who drank beer while repeating the few phrases of a strange English they had borrowed like the dresses they used to lure their men, gave the men diseases in exchange for dollar bills. He had listened to the stories unable to laugh, as if the need to laugh originated in a delicate crisis that flared when a slowly squeezed trigger lost its balance and exploded the mechanism needing only a thin impulse to uncoil itself. And there was a yellow smell that never went away, sometimes passing into troubled sleep.

He wondered what the huddled group of villagers thought of him as he walked from hut to hut, his hand always ready on the pistol holstered at his side. But he did not know how he ended up where he did, and what urge possessed him to require the old woman to watch. He saw two soldiers push a young girl into a hut, and remembered thinking yes, the stories are true. And suddenly he found himself in another hut with the boy and the old woman, she at first whimpering until he slapped her across the face, the boy silent, his eyes vacant and hard.

He quickly looked around—the dirt floors and crude wooden table and chairs, an open bag of rice, clay pots and a tin pan. Even then he did not know what he would do. He pushed the old woman down in a corner and forced the boy away from her toward the wall made of flattened tin cans. As he tightened his grip on his pistol and saw the boy's eyes open wide, the old woman lowered her head to the floor. Then he drew the pistol out with its barrel and lifted the boy's chin up toward him.

He looked around once more to see everything—for to see everything again confirmed that it had not all happened in some dark, dim dream—and as his eyes wandered about the hut he returned to the old woman in the corner, whose eyes stared beyond the wall near which he stood.

In a different space and time he had met a different woman, Mrs. Festerson. In the supermarket behind a grocery basket heaped high with boxes and cans. They talked about the weather, about the reporter who came to her house. The next day he saw her name in the *Daily News*:

> "Mrs. Festerson explained . . . she has mixed emotions about the December bombing blitz . . . But I really think . . . something to bring Hanoi to its knees . . . but in the long run . . . She does not believe . . . the U.S. should intervene again . . . it should be in the form of . . . rather than more of our boys . . ."

He saw her smile and say thank you. She gave him a polite good-day, then pushed her grocery basket down the aisle as if she was happy now that it was full of solid opinions. In the corner of the hut, the old woman, her eyes beyond conviction or accusation in their steady stare beyond him and beyond the walls of the hut, sat with her back humped wearily toward the ground.

He ordered the boy to his knees, waited for him to obey. Instead the boy stood his ground. When he grabbed the boy by the hair and wrestled him down, the boy yielded, not struggling except to turn his face up.

Breaths came in short heaves as a hand began fumbling at a zipper. The boy closed his eyes and turned his head away, avoiding even the face of the old woman. The soldier grabbed the hair behind the boy's forehead and twisted his head back, until the boy looked up with begging eyes. Then he struck the boy sharply across the side of the face, sending him sprawling across the dirt floor of the hut.

"You pay? You pay?" the boy asked, half-glancing at the old woman.

This time the soldier half-screamed in rage as he struck the boy across the side of the head with his open hand. "You goddamn money-fucking nigger-gooks!"

The boy drew himself up straight-backed this time, like an altar-boy serving a priest. Their eyes met for a moment, then darted apart.

"Do it!" he screamed at the boy. "Just do it!"

He did not see the confusion begin to clear from the boy's face as the soldier's meaning became clear. He looked down at the boy and saw that his eyes were closed. The boy did not look up, so the soldier looked away, groped for other thoughts, pleasant thoughts.

She came into view standing in an orange bikini on the brown sand, tall and warm and tanned, mouthing a sweating bottle of Pepsi Cola. I will pour it in your bikini and lick it, he said, and she said yes, yes in a whisper close to his lips, and then she laughed as she went high-stepping away, twirling a baton before thousands in a stadium. He watched her as she crossed a field. For a long minute he swayed with the rhythm of her hips and stared into the small space where her legs met. Around him everyone was screaming, but he was small and quiet in the crowd. He hated the crowd, the people, their mad screaming for no good reason at all, and he would not stand when they stood. He would sit quietly and wait until she came back for him. He was not crazy. He would never play football like those fools did.

Then suddenly she appeared again. He saw her at the end of the game walking out with number eighty-seven, the nigger lineman from Louisiana, the big nigger laughing as he let his hand slide down her ass, and she squiggling as she smiled up at the crowd while he, a lost face, wondered what this world was coming to.

His wife screamed at him. Would he please scrub the burn marks from the pan? No, leave me alone, you bitch. When's your next leave? Not for another six months? Oh I love you my dear, my darling. Good-bye. And even, almost, a tear as he walked toward the waiting plane, a tear as he looked back at her and waved. The airport looked like a tidy flat model from the air. Nothing like the shacks and strange smells in the back streets of Saigon. Then a pounding in his head, a furious driving back and forth. You've got to let yourself go once in a while, they told him. Four years, he thought, and now this. It had come to this. He had heard, but never, never did he think he. But he was free now. No longer afraid. It's the ultimate, they told him. How do you know? Degrading, he told them. The ultimate degradation. Degrading. The whole war's degrading. It puts you on their level. They're pigs. Yellow pigs. Never would I.

And soon he could say he touched me, oh how wonderful, he touched me. The yellow pig. He remembered how his wife sighed the first time he put his hand on her breast when they were parked near the high school. Lock the doors, she told him, because they say there's niggers cruising in these streets at night. After white girls. They don't like their own kind. Fuck them. Fuck them before they fuck you. Yes, lock the doors. I'll do anything you say if you lock the doors.

And years later he didn't care anymore. The niggers were moving closer and nobody said a word. One even started coming to his church, and no one said a word. He had white hair and a gray pinstriped suit. He didn't look like a nigger until he smiled. Then you could see that his teeth were small. He smiled at everyone and the first day he came to the church he thrust his hand at everyone. No one said a word even after they saw him sitting near the front of the church, and one Sunday he was on the platform with everyone else. No one said a word because it got out that he gave ten percent to the church, and he had plenty. He came from somewhere in the South, they said.

It didn't matter to him anymore after that, because he knew that money could get you anywhere. He never listened to the preacher anymore, but only watched the preacher's wife, the soloist, who had big breasts and who, when she sang about Jesus, smiled as if he had spent the night with her. Almost every other Sunday, it seemed, she sang her favorite hymn, her eyes closed and her chest heaving with the hymn's last line: "He touched me, O how wonderful, he touched me."

It was a Baptist church, a low flat building made of painted cinder blocks, but there no longer was anywhere for the people to sit and the pastor said the Lord would see to it that they soon might be moving downtown to the big stone church once owned by the Presbyterians. He used to watch the melancholy in the preacher's wife's face pass as her eyes followed the words of the hymn fading from her, rising up toward the squares of tile that lined the low ceiling of the room the preacher insisted on calling the tabernacle. He had touched her, and she had felt it in her arms, breasts, lungs, and voice, all of them quivering with conviction, and, at the moment she lost herself in the song, with joy.

He had never felt that. He had never felt the conviction or the joy. During all the months he had been in the war he had only waited and moved about his duties as if in a foul-smelling dream. He had seen some of the dead, but death never would touch him. The men they brought in piled in the back of trucks were dirty and torn, and flies swarmed on their eyes and mouths. But he kept himself clean and the soloist's bosom was clean. She was one woman he would not dare touch.

And he remembered what happened right after he talked to Mrs. Festerson. Right in the supermarket parking lot. The nigger boy who threw himself at his feet and started to chatter while shining his shoes and rubbing the spit into them. And before he could walk away from the boy, he was trapped, late with the groceries. They wouldn't make the early show. As the boy shined and shined, spitting on his shoe, the chatter faded and the smile straightened. He wanted to kick him, do anything to get away, but there were people around. And when the boy, kneeling on a matted pad spread before him, looked up, the smile was gone.

"Two dolla, suh!"

He felt no rage now. The hut was too small to contain anything more than a memory of the madness that came over him when he not only could not refuse to pay but had to wait while the boy fumbled through a fat roll of bills, counting out eighteen singles to change the twenty dollar bill he had to give him. And now in the hut he could smile because he was getting his money's worth. He had seen the justice of it in the eyes of the preacher's wife. He remembered again how her voice quivered slightly as she sang the last line of the chorus for the last time. "He touched me, Oh how wonderful, He touched me." The words rose from deep within her and floated over heads bowed in sorrow and prayer.

"And now come," he heard the preacher say. "All of you out there who have been touched, come. Come, kneel at the altar and offer yourself to Jesus. With every head bowed and every eye closed, I want you weary sinners to come." And as he thought about the voice begging him to come forth, he saw the preacher with his arms outstretched facing not the congregation but the wall behind the altar. He could not see the preacher's face, recognize his voice. But he stood up and walked toward the front. "Come, you sinners," the preacher shouted once more, his back still turned.

Yes. It was time to give himself up. He felt his body giving in. He felt himself swaying now, and he let himself go. His whole body rose in that moment, and then he felt the rush again. Suddenly, as if his eyes opened as his heart skipped a beat, he saw himself in the hut, with its Pepsi Cola wall, the boy on his knees, and the old woman crumbled in a corner, her face turned away. In that moment he realized that nothing could stop him from surrendering or stop the rush that sent him running toward the platform, toward the preacher whose back was turned, and who whirled, showing him a black face with small teeth, the preacher who screamed like a wild man as he spread a pain as sharp as a spear through the room.

The pain spread through his body, and there was no more past, only the hut and the woman screaming, the boy still on his knees, and he vainly trying to fend the boy off with his hand as if the boy were a dog. Then the rush and the pain ended with the crack of the pistol, which his hand had wrestled from his holster. For a moment the boy seemed to hang suspended in the air as blood spurted over his face. He saw the boy's eyes in a last desperate moment asking why, and then everything collapsed as the boy fell to the floor of the hut.

There was no thought, only the pain and the blood. As his hand fumbled again for his zipper he saw, as he drew it away, his own blood on it.

The old woman in the corner had lifted her face, and as he ran out she began the old ritual wail for the dead, slow and quiet, warning everyone that sorrow was wandering the countryside again. The villagers had heard the wail before, so when the·soldiers left they would leave their places of hiding to wail with the old woman beside their dead.

ENEMY COUNTRY

Tony never looked the Italian lady in the eye. He never looked anyone in the eye, so he never saw anyone making fun of him. He never looked anyone in the eye because he was sure that if he did they would discover his hiding place.

The old lady was the only one who never accused. *Filio mio*, she called him, my son. But he never knew what to say in return. His real mother, dead seven years, was a plain woman who cried too much except the last month when it was clear, even to Tony's father, that she was ready to die. Then suddenly she was gone, leaving dirty dishes in the sink. This woman who called Tony her son was older but stood more straight. From the bushes he saw her appear at the back door when it was time to send her man to work at the Ford plant for the midnight shift. She loaded him down with a big brown-bag lunch and thermos full of coffee and milk, then waited at the window until the bus stopped for him. In two years, she said, he could retire with a gold watch. The pension and Social Security would get them by from day to day.

When the bus arrived each night Tony made sure the man got on. Then he came out from his hiding place, walked to the house and stood on the back step, the coffee, still hot, waiting for him inside. Each night he sat stooped over the kitchen table surrounding the cup in his big awkward hands, breathing in the black aroma while she explained about a sister in Highland Park, the price of ground beef, or the reason the bread did not turn out just right.

"Missus," he said one night, "I think something's the matter with me. I'm losing my hair. Every day I get up and I look like I'm bald."

"No, no, no," she said, touching his shoulder. "Nothing the matter. No worry. You looking more like a baby to me."

Then one day she could not ignore his eyes and hands. "You be in the war, no? They ruin you over there. I know because they ruin my boy. Now he gone. He have eyes like you, but he never go out at night."

He never stayed long with the Italian lady. She washed the dishes and drank coffee too, always had cake or cookies to offer him. "You make the best coffee, Missus," he said. "I never had coffee like this." He caressed the steaming hot cup and held it close to his face, looking not at her or anywhere except down into the cup, the coffee in it swirling like a bottomless black well. She kept filling it until the pot on the old white stove was empty. By then she had less to say. There were long silences until he, who rarely said more than yes or no, finally whispered thank you, thank you Missus, put his cap on his balding head, and went out by the kitchen door in back.

Tony's father, who seemed like an old man even to him, never went out at night. He had been in two wars and was always full of words, knew the names of senators, baseball players, mayors and generals, and every morning complained until he walked out the door and past the rows of small neat houses to the shelter at the park to play cards with the other retired factory men. And when he returned just before dark he always complained again. "Tony, you still in your room? Jesus Christ, Tony. You can't stay in your room all day. Why don't you go out? Why don't you get a job? Why don't you clean the house?"

When Tony was sure his father was asleep, he went out.

He went through the back yard into the alley, where he crouched behind a bush by the corner of the fence and watched the old lady through the window until she closed the curtains, turned off the lights and faded away into the darkness of the house. Then he stood up and walked the two blocks to the lumber yard. There he climbed over the fence along the railroad tracks and walked east toward the river across from which he could see the Canadian shore, a place he had never been, where the cowards hid. Just past the lumber yard he walked through the neighborhood where he was born, the small city blocks jammed with wooden houses, all of them old, leaning askew, all exuding a musty smell that seemed to come up from the basements to hover at night over the wood and junk piled in stacks in back yards along the tracks.

The old neighborhood gave way to the warehouses. For almost a mile Tony passed empty brick buildings with broken windows. Then he passed the Edison power plant with its piles of coal, and the tracks led through an open field near the oil refinery, its strange towers and eerie flames reminding him of church. Finally he came to the river itself, a half mile wide but quiet and black except for dull glares that shimmered off the water from the few lights along the opposite shore.

Even in the cold Tony spent long hours by the river. He found a pile of concrete slabs dumped in the weeds along the shore, and he climbed to the top of them to a place where he could sit and lean back against a flat piece, dangling his feet in the air over the water. Here he sat looking downriver into the black water and at the dirty yellow haze hovering around the city lights to the south. At the first sign of dawn his body jerked him into motion again, down the pile of concrete slabs and back up the railroad tracks to his house. Tony felt good along the way back until he heard the

4:20 express bearing down toward him, and, a full mile before the train passed him, he groped in panic around the side of the tracks for a pile of wood or a bush to crouch behind until the train went screaming away down the tracks.

Then he returned to his house—to the small bedroom where he sat in a chair in a darkened corner waiting for the sun, climbing into bed where he pretended to sleep when his father, before leaving the house for his game of cards at the park, looked in to see if he was back.

Usually he lay curled in bed an hour or two, the shades drawn, sleep refusing him. He wondered if he would die, putting his hand next to his heart so he could feel the pulse. He was better now, because there was a time when he was afraid of his sergeant too, and of the soldier who shot the boy in the face. It happened during his second patrol, so he remembered it all—the Phantoms passing over and the explosions that became visible over the tops of trees, the slow walk toward the village that turned into a run, a mad sprint past the thicket and into the village, the rattling of automatics as everyone ran randomly among the huts until they saw the villagers huddled together outside one of the huts; the dead boy lying at the door of the hut, his face lost in a pool of blood that was still draining from his head, the soldier nervously fumbling with his pants with one hand while trying to re-holster his pistol with the other, and the old Vietnamese woman on her knees who wailed and wailed next to the dead boy's body.

And two days later at the poker game he heard the soldier explain. It was early in the night but the soldier, drunk, had won four hands in a row and had gathered the chips from the last hands around him with his arms. He rolled an unlit cigar in his mouth while studying the cards. He laughed at everything, and his laughter filled the room. Tony leaned in closer to see if the soldier would say anything about what he heard everyone else talk about, and a few others dropped their cards on the table and listened close. The soldier had nothing to say to any of them before, but they'd better listen once and for all. He was so goddamn mad, he said, that one night he came within a second of fragging his own C.O. There was no need for a fuss, no need for him to answer anybody's questions. What he did was all in the line of duty and nobody's business, and nobody had a right to start trouble with him. The gook had a gun and was going to kill him as soon as his sister gave him the signal, and he saw the gun even though the sergeant said the kid had no gun, because after the kid attacked him and was shot he never looked at him again or searched for the gun but ran out of the hut to find help. And really it was the boy's sister's fault because she wanted to do it for a price, right then and there in the middle of the attack, and he of course said hell no and slapped her and that's when she screamed and grabbed his hand and bit it and gave the signal for the boy to shoot him, but he was too quick and saw it coming and turned real quick-like and with one shot brought the gook down. And the bitch she just sank down in a corner of the hut behind a table and hid, and he walked over to her and wanted to shoot her too because it was her fault, but then he suddenly felt sorry for her in that degraded condition and sorry for all her people too because of this miserable war, so he let her lie and just left to call for help. And later, when an old woman complained to a village chief that he had forced her to watch, she was just making up a story to make the Americans look bad. And that is the way it happened, he said as he picked up his cards for one last hand, and he didn't like the C.O. calling him to talk about it, even though later they agreed it was nothing to worry about because everybody knows the gooks are everywhere.

Tony remembered being more confused when he heard this, and he knew then why he would never be able to be one of them, why he would sit near the window and watch them play poker but never be able to play, never be smart enough to make jokes the way they did, not have the guts to be soldiers like them. For the soldier's story was almost like the one that everyone said was true, but Tony thought there must be something wrong with his mind because he was there and he saw different things. He didn't see any gun and the boy wasn't a gook because he was only nine or ten, and he didn't see the boy's sister hiding behind the table or anyone else except the old woman, because he was the one who went in, found the old lady kneeling by the boy wailing, and led her out of the hut to her own people. And he could not understand what the soldier was doing in the middle of the hut with his pants halfway down and a gun in his hands.

Every time he thought about it he only got more confused, and it was too bad because when he got home there was no one to ask, not even the Italian lady, who probably hadn't heard about it and would say it's just one of those things.

He had no idea what caused him to hide in the corner of one of the toilet stalls until they found him and carried him to the brig. He felt a terrible confusion that every night moved down from his head to his chest, the feeling he had as a boy when he climbed a tall tree along the river shore from where he could see all the river's wide blue expanse and the other shore which had no factories but green areas that looked like woods, a good feeling until he looked down and saw how high he was and suddenly was sure he would fall and break his legs. And when he came down from the tree his legs were so scared he could barely walk, just as he could barely stand before roll call that morning when he slipped away and hid, crouched in the corner of the toilet stall where his legs caved in and his voice failed when they discovered and carried him away.

They let him out in three days and he tried to be by himself, but they wouldn't leave him alone.

"Hey Tony, you want to play. Come on over here, Tony, and we'll let you play." The soldier who said this was the mechanic. He had one eye closed and with the other he squinted at his cards through the smoke.

"Come on, Tony. Come over here."

So he moved closer to watch not the cards or the game but the eyes of the men who sat there each night talking of nothing but the women and the boozing and the blacks who sat together on the other side of the room sulking like overfed cats in a cage. And once, just once, he thought maybe I belong over there with them, and he looked over his shoulder just in time to see one of the blacks put his hand over his mouth to keep from laughing out loud.

"They're laughing at you Tony," whispered the mechanic so everyone could hear. "The niggers are laughing at you. You going to let them laugh at you?"

Everyone waited for him to move, but there was nothing he could do. He looked down at the floor.

"Deal," the mechanic said. "Deal me a queen of spades." He shuffled the cards, handed them to Tony. "Seven card stud. Spades are wild."

Everyone laughed as Tony dished out the cards, the laughter thrown backward over their shoulders like glances at the blacks on the other side of the room. Then a silence as everyone studied the cards in their hands.

"Hey, I only got six cards," the mechanic said. He picked a peanut from the table and threw it point-blank at Tony's face. "Don't you know how to count, you stupid gook?"

Tony appealed to the blacks as he made his way to the door, but they had turned their backs to everything in the room.

He never forgot that, or forgave, because he never would forget what happened two days before he decided to try hiding in the toilet stall. They were on patrol, seven of them, two of them blacks, more than a mile from the base. They had been in these woods maybe a dozen times before, but they never took the same path, and they all thought they would just go back the way they always did and play cards again.

The C.O. once had to stop to lecture them about the whispering and carrying on. "This is enemy country, you fools," he hissed. "Everyone's enemy country here." So all of them except Tony pretended to be serious, laughing behind the C.O.'s back and giving him the finger until the fun wore out and they all noticed there suddenly was no breeze or noise of any kind except their own thrashing through the brush, and they all became a little afraid. Then they heard the shells over their heads, two of them, and Tony covered his head with his arms and threw himself down at the foot of a large tree. He was lifted off the ground by more blasts, branches and dirt falling on him, one heavy stone striking the side of his kneecap and a pain coming from there so terrible it paralyzed his legs. For a second he raised his head to look for the other men, but he saw nothing but trees all broken apart. He wanted to run and he somehow would have run but he heard another shell coming in and he curled himself up with his knees drawn up to his chest and his arms around his head until it landed, this time farther away and to his left. He heard a branch cracking overhead and found himself running like a crazy man, this time not hitting the ground each time he heard the shells and knowing only that they were exploding in front of him no matter which way he ran. He thought that the earth itself would never stop shaking under him, and without knowing it he found that he had stopped running and was standling alone on some grass surrounded by splintered trees. It was then that the blinding pain in his knee made him sit down. As he sat down next to a bush he felt everything give way, his legs and arms and whatever clear sense was left in his mind. Then as suddenly as the noises began a silence and the sunshine of late morning fell on him. But those few seconds were shattered by shouts in front of him, then big gunfire, nervous, persistent, out of control. So he crouched and waited, trying to choke down sobs that convulsed his chest.

He crouched down lower because he heard them coming his way. They were not making any sound with their feet but rustling bushes as they passed from one tree to another toward him, their bodies all shadow even in the streaks of sun that found their way to the forest floor. "Gooks," his mind whispered to him, "these are gooks, gooks, gooks."

He turned his head as if to ask the mechanic if it was true, but the mechanic was not there. In that moment he saw himself standing straight up, screaming at them to turn his way, then shooting them with everything he had, his dizzy fire finished only when all the fury in him saw them coming closer and closer to the bush that hid him. Then he went limp, awkward behind the bush, his eyes fixed on the hands that in panic had thrown his weapon away. And all the time his heart beat louder and louder, as if it wanted to give him away.

They passed close, almost close enough to hear him breathe, and he counted them one by one, his mind whispering gooks, gooks, gooks even while his eyes saw that these were boys, their faces weary and sad and their eyes, like his, terrified.

When the recovery team found him that afternoon even the medics laughed at him for not being able to walk. There was only a slight swelling in the knee, they said, but nothing to write home about. They carried him in on a stretcher, dumped him in the barracks, and told him to wash. He heard all the talk. "Hey Tony, they say you got scared, run like a scared rabbit. And there was only one of them, Tony, only one gook. Couple of them black dudes got him good. Shot him right in the head."

Instead of washing he crawled to his bed and pulled the blanket over his head until the C.O. came by later that night and ordered him to shower and shave. When this happened he wasn't crying any more or shaking. He never said a word but his eyes danced more wildly than they ever had before.

He didn't know why they shipped him home and it did not matter to him. Once they carried him out of the toilet stall he did not care what they did to him any more. At first they asked him questions he could not answer

54

and then ones he could, but he decided not to say a word because he wasn't going to give any secrets away. They sent him back to the barracks, but he did not care, especially when it came time for him to get on the truck that carried him away from them.

Carried him back home, that is, to the old man who was his father, the room he kept locked all day, and the lady who gave him black coffee before he walked alone down the tracks to the river every night.

At first his father wanted him to go to Canada, to Windsor across the river where he knew a man who owned a restaurant, or to Minnesota, where he could work in the mines with a cousin. He was a hero from the war, his father said, so somebody would give him a job. But Tony said no, he wanted to stay in his room, only cowards went to Canada. He told his father to leave him alone, because he would go out whenever he felt like going out.

For a few weeks he tried—always at night. As soon as night fell he followed alleys to Michigan Avenue, where he lost himself on the sidewalks with the others wandering the streets. There was a certain downtown street that had a special allure. It was a short street no more than three blocks long facing the backs of some of the tallest buildings downtown. He liked this street because the shops stayed open all night and because no one here would stare at him. Here signs made out of blinking lightbulbs said "DANCING," with an arrow pointing up dark stairs, and barroom doors opened to jukeboxes singing love songs to men on the streets, and there was a penny arcade on one corner with slot machines where Tony would stop to spend some of the small change his father gave him every other day. And there was a bookstore, a quiet place, loaded with old used books, the neat sets always on top out of reach, and piles of paperbacks for sale for a nickel or dime, and magazines full of picture of half-naked girls. This was the place Tony liked best of all.

The man who owned this store, a small Oriental who stared out the window and smoked, never asked Tony's name. "The Chinaman," Tony called him. He always nodded when Tony came in as if to let him know he was being watched, but once, abandoning his place by the window, he picked out a book for Tony to read. Tony took the book home that night and read eight pages before falling asleep, and the next night went back and asked the man to pick out another one for him.

It was what happened a week later in that same bookshop that caused Tony never to go back. He arrived later that night, and the shopkeeper had turned the lights out in the back room. Tony saw two men standing out front when he entered the shop, and he noticed them looking in at the row of fancy girly magazines the shopkeeper displayed in the center of the window. When Tony looked up from the pages of a magazine, he saw the tall one—a lanky black in a marine corps jacket and bandana around his hair— standing over the counter talking to the shopkeeper. "You a motherfucking cheat," the black man said. Then he saw the black bend over the counter and look down at the shopkeeper, whose face quivered when he tried to speak. Tony shrank away, trying not to hear yet turning sideways so he could see. But in less than a minute the business in the room was his, for he heard what started the argument and without knowing it nodded toward the shopkeeper his support, almost at the very same moment that he saw the shorter one—this one more light-skinned with almost reddish hair and a fancy pink shirt—leaning against the bookcase just inside the door watching him. Tony lowered the magazine he was holding and turned to watch the two men argue about the girly book that the tall black now held behind his back. "Two dollah, suh?" The tall black screamed the words at the shopkeeper, who stepped back from the counter and stared silently beyond the screaming man at the books on the opposite wall. "I give you fifty cents!" the tall black began shouting over and over at the man. The shopkeeper stood unmoved, his head slightly rocking back and forth but saying firmly and finally no, no deal, not now or later or next year or even when I am dead. And Tony too was shaking his head, not so much in agreement with the shopkeeper but as if to say it was all too bad, it was all some bad mistake and didn't have to be, and why did it happen here where he came every night to leave all that behind. Then suddenly the shorter one with the slick red hair and pink shirt was inside, shouting orders at the taller one. "You kill 'em now, boy! You kill 'em both!" The tall black paused, wavered where he stood as if a heavy confusion was passing away, leaving in its place a clearing and a light, a justification for performing the act that had never occurred to him before the short one put him up to it.

"You a gook," he said, glaring in surprise at the shopkeeper. Then as he turned to face Tony the full assurance came to his dancing eyes. "You a gook too! You *both* gooks!"

The short one tried to trip him as Tony ran out the door into the street. When Tony ran around the corner where the arcade was he did not notice that most of the lights had been turned off and that the city streets were empty and dark. He ran without looking back until he thought his heart would give out, turning into alleys he had never seen before. He had entered a long narrow alley bounded on both sides by the high brick walls of warehouses, and the alley took him away until he knew he could no longer run. Over his shoulder he saw two shadows turn the corner toward him. But his legs were too heavy to run, and his knee ached. He turned into a short alley that branched both left and right, and pausing as if to let his mind make the choice, he turned right and ran again. He ran as fast as he could, then hurled himself face down behind three garbage cans.

Two hours passed before he lifted himself up, shivering from the cold. "What you do here?" a small voice asked from behind. "You wanna cuppa coffee? You wanna come inside?"

He surrendered to her, let her lead him away by the arm. He said nothing at first, refused to give any secrets away. But then he saw she wanted nothing from him, so he found words and made her promise one thing:

"Sure, sure," she said, "you just say."

"Don't tell anybody I'm hiding here."

So he went back again and again, each night climbing over the fence at the lumber yard and walking down the railroad tracks to the river and back after finishing his coffee and waiting in the bushes for her to turn off the lights.

This is what Tony did until one night he walked to the back door and waited as he always did. The old lady's sister, eyeing him up and down, told him she was in the hospital. He knew then by the sister's face that the old lady would never be back. Somehow it didn't seem right any more to crouch behind the fence waiting for the lights to go off and the curtains to close so he could be sure she was safe, or to walk down the tracks to the river and the concrete slabs where he could see across the river to Canada, so he said nothing and returned to his room in his father's house.

"What am I going to do with you, Tony," his father complained. "You don't want to work. You never go out of your room. What am I going to do with you?"

Tony said nothing, but he had made up his mind. I have a gun, he told himself. I have it hidden in my room, and I have a good hiding place. I have a bed and a dresser full of clothes with my mother's picture on it, and I have a closet too. If they try to come in here they'll be sorry, sorry. If the niggers try to get in here, I'll kill every one. I swear I'll kill every one.

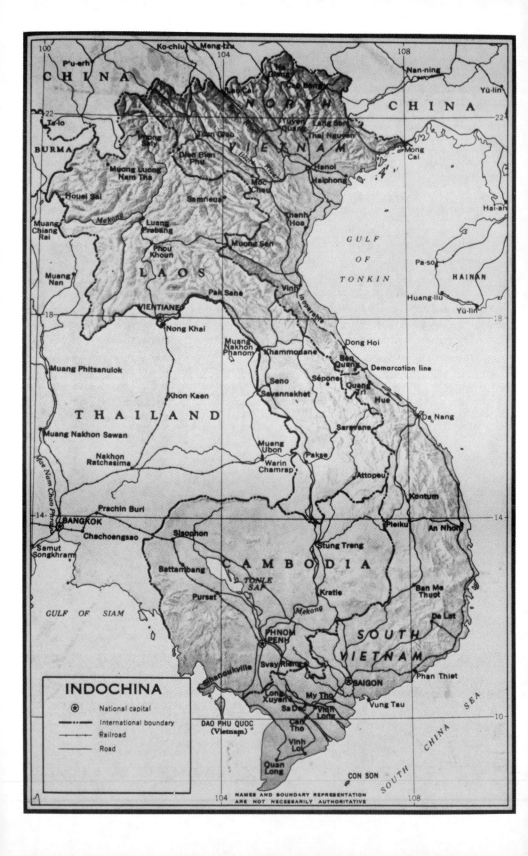

BROTHERS OF THE TIGER

On a warm morning just four months after the celebration of Tet, Nguyen Be, a peasant born in the northern village of Lai Chan, set out on foot with a mule and cart from a wooden shack on the outskirts of Dien Bien Phu. His desination was My Tho, a village in the Mekong Delta beyond Saigon far to the south. In this village Nguyen Be had a gravely ill younger brother, Hong, a farmer and tender of a small orchard. Nguyen Be had not seen his brother in ten years, and he was fearful that if he did not go now he never again would see him alive. On the mule cart the old man carried a few days' provisions—a sack of rice, a pot for boiling it, some charcoal, a bagful of oats and some carrots for his mule, and a blanket to sleep on.

Before the old man had gone more than a mile down the narrow road leading from his shack, he spoke to his mule and they both stopped by the side of the road. Over the ridge ahead the yellow veil of morning began forming into a thin cloud. As the sun showed itself above the trees lining the ridge, a few beams broke through the leaves and began warming the road ahead of the travellers. By noon the yellow veil would be a cloud sealing in thick heat. The mule pawed the ground, took two steps back, and turned toward the high grass along the road where in the reeds he found a small rivulet running along the road. Startled, two small birds flew up from the nearby grass, and as the old man lifted his head toward the sun to watch them go, they skimmed the top of the high grass, and, weaving a tighter pattern as they rose, disappeared into dots against the yellow veil over the ridge. When he could no longer see the flight of the birds, he sat down cross-legged on the roadside and pulled his hat down to shade his face. The mule, still tied to the wooden cart, slumped down sleepy-eyed next to the old man and nosed for tender shoots.

Scraping clean the bowl of a long wooden pipe with a sharp stone, the old man glanced upward as if watching for the return of the birds. He lit the pipe, offered it to the mule, who turned his nose up at it, and then drew the smoke deeply in, letting his whole body sink down as he let it out. A breeze stirred as he exhaled, and the smoke was swiftly carried away. The mule tried the air a moment, then lowered his head and closed his eyes, and together the two of them sat motionless.

A mosquito hovering near the old man's head finally landed on his hand and stung the calm. The old man flicked it away and saw a small black figure far down the road. He took another deep draw from his pipe, held the smoke in, and watched as the figure approached. Shimmering in the waves of heat rising from the road, the figure slowly came into view, as if rising out of a pond of bright water.

Nguyen Be nodded when the figure, a youth of about fifteen years carrying a bundle of sticks on his shoulders, stood over him.

"A good morning to you, Nguyen Be. I see you have begun your journey to your brother in the south."

Nguyen Be nodded again.

"At this rate," the boy laughed, "you won't get there until the next Tet."

Nguyen Be glanced backward down the road. "Where are you going with your sticks?"

"Where you came from," the boy said. "I bring them to my mother there."

"Then you slow down. Even a boy like you can lose all his breath if he hurries too fast. And the midday sun is on the rise."

"But I'll be there long before the sun is up," he said.

"Will you be there before I finish my journey to the south?"

"Ha," said the youth, "you're not even to Ban Cang yet, and I doubt you will get there by the middle of the night."

The mule opened one eye, circled the scene once, and closed it again.

"You had better sit and smoke with me," the old man said. "I do not have many breaths left in my days, so the ones I take must be long and slow."

The boy smiled, slipped the bundle off his back, and sat down before the old man. Already the old man had refilled and lit the pipe, and he handed it to the boy.

In the southeastern sky the cloud had formed, but it carried with it no promise of rain. And as the youth drew the smoke in for the first time, the two birds startled from the grass had found their way back to their nest only a few feet away from the mule.

*   *   *   *

Chronology of the G464 Demolition Unit of the My Tho Province 415th Local Force Battalion

April 29, 1966: Request from the demolition unit's Party Chapter to the battalion for additional men to strengthen the unit to seventeen.

May 4, 1966: Three-month training course for the demolition unit initiated.

June 16, 1966: Conference of all cadres in the battalion to discuss the new political mission set forth by the Battalion Party Committee.

June 27, 1966: Planning for attack on Hao Ninh.

July 18, 1966: Battalion assigned a new operation by the Province Military Affairs Section.

July 29, 1966: Meeting of all political and military cadres in the battalion to discuss the attack on "K-89," or Giong Trom village. There are not records of the attack taking place.

Aug. 11, 1966: Unit strength down to 13 men. Demolition unit commander requests reinforcements.

Sept., 1966: Two months of training scheduled.

Oct., 1966: Unit strength totals 19 men, 17 present for duty.

Nov. 15, 1966: Indoctrination to launch 3rd Phase of Activities.

Jan. 9, 1967: Six-day training program initiated with emphasis on political training.

Feb. 7, 1967: Battalion in bivouac for Tet.

Feb. 21, 1967: Twenty-six day training program ordered by the Battalion Command Staff.

March 30, 1967: All battalion cadres discuss "K-136" and "K-114" military plans.

April 13, 1967: New additions to the demolition unit. Active strength remains at 17.

April 29, 1967: Political indoctrination on the role of all cadres.

May 1, 1967: Another plan of attack on "K-141" and "K-13B" is disseminated.

May 14, 1967: Evaluation of the spring campaign.

May 19, 1967: Orders given for "deep and systematic penetration into enemy areas of pacification." May 22, 1967: Meeting of all Company Command Staffs and Battalion Command Staff.

May 29, 1967: Eighteen-day training schedule begins.

June 3, 1967: Defense against an enemy sweep action in Cho Gao village.

July 17, 1967: Attack by the unit on Tan An village.

Aug. 13-19, 1967: Series of encounters with US-GVN forces near My Tho village culminate in the loss of demolition unit documents.

DOCUMENT NO. 1

List of Members of G464 Demolition Unit of 415th Local Force Battalion

Real Name	Alias	DOB	Height	Health	Marks
Hau My	Viet Phuoc	1945	1.55m	A	scar on belly
Ap Moi	Le Thanh	1943	1.55m	B	
Duc Hua	Ninh Hong	1942	1.65m	B	
Trang Bang	Tran Viet	1941	1.65m	B	
Ben Cat	Le Hong Duc	1942	1.60m	A	scar on forehead
Hieu Liem	Van Tam	1946	1.55m	B	
Gia Kiem	Hong Minh	1942	1.55m	B	
Ba Gieng	Thanh Son	1943	1.65m	B	
Lam Kuan	Tran Ba	1949	1.60m	B	scar on face (right side)
Hung Nhon	Nguyen Xe	1944	1.55m	A	
Nuoc Ngot	Ha Kiet	1946	1.50m	A	scar on belly
Thong Nhot	Ha Manh	1940	1.55m	B	pock-marked face
Dong Hoa	Ha Van Be	1945	1.65m	B	
Thua Duc	Ngo Hiep	1943	1.60m	A	scar on buttocks
Ba Tri	Truong Ho	1944	1.55m	B	scar on chin
Vung Liem	Son Thoai	1947	1.55m	B	
Binh Minh	Nguyen Son	1941	1.60m	B	
Cat Mon	Cai Tho	1943	1.70m	A	scar over right eye
Giao Duc	Ha Muoi	1945	1.55m	B	

Education	Family Class.	Property	Function
illiterate	poor farmer	2 mau of land (distributed by revolution)	deputy squad leader
3rd year	poor farmer		fighter
3rd year	poor farmer	8 cong 1 radio	squad leader
2nd year	poor farmer		fighter
illiterate	new middle farmer	1 mau 1 sampan	squad leader
	poor farmer	1 mau	deputy squad leader
literate	poor farmer		cell leader
	poor farmer		fighter
	poor farmer	rent 3 cong	fighter
2nd year	very poor farmer	1 mau (distributed)	fighter
3rd year	poor farmer	10 cong (distributed)	assistant squad leader
illiterate	poor farmer	15 cong (distributed)	fighter
3rd year	very poor farmer		fighter
	poor farmer	1 mau (distributed)	squad leader
literate	poor farmer	7 cong (distributed) 1 pump	fighter
2nd year	very poor farmer	2 buffalos	assistant squad leader
	poor farmer	1 mau 1 sewing machine	fighter
3rd year	poor farmer	3 cong 1 pump	fighter
2nd year	poor farmer		assistant squad leader

POEM

From a Notebook of Cat Mon: Member of
the G464 Demolition Unit of the My Tho Province
415th Local Force Battalion

Autumn passes away, winter comes, and then spring returns.
I am as always enraptured by my mission.
Before me, flowers bloom in brilliant colors in front of
    someone's house,
A bamboo branch sways gracefully, reminding me of your
    native village.
Our unit stops to rest in an isolated area.
My shoes are still covered with dust gathered during
    the march.
I hurriedly compose this letter to you
And send you all my love.

The Veto-Incremax Procedure:
POTENTIAL FOR VIETNAM CONFLICT RESOLUTION

There are several possible veto-incremax procedures. (Incremax is an abbreviation for incremental maximization, and involves a maximization process taken over each of a series of small steps.) Each has the following appealing features:

(1) each can be presented in a relatively simple form for a given situation, and can be rigorously defined mathematically;

(2) each gives each participant a full veto power which he may exercise at any time, and assures each participant that he will end no worse off than at the start if any participant does exercise his veto power:

(3) each clearly points up the inefficiency of the existing position (deadlock, threat point, current-stand point or prominent reference point) and identifies a common goal (the achievement of a mutually preferred outcome which is efficient);

(4) each requires that each participant be able to state consistently his preferences among outcomes. Thus, each depends on no intercomparisons of utility, and only requires the assumption of ordinal utility;

(5) each assures that no participant will ever be made worse off on any move, except by the exercise of the veto power;

(6) each allows each participant to be as conservative and cautious as he desires with respect to the amount of change in proposed actions on any move; that is, within extreme limits, each participant is allowed to make as small a commitment on change as he desires;

(7) provided the veto power is not exercised, each insures that an efficient outcome will be reached, but that no participant is able beforehand to idenfity the specific set of changes in the joint proposals, or steps, required to achieve that outcome;

(8) each suggests a "fair compromise" or "equitable" procedure by which all participants may share in the gains from the gradual advancement to a mutually more efficient state of affairs;

(9) each allows participants considerable flexibility in combining its appealing features with the appealing features of several other veto-incremax procedures into a single synthesized procedure.

More formally, we may proceed to state the general properties of veto-incremax procedures as follows:

Property (1) VETO POWER. On any move the procedure allows each participant to exercise the veto power, which exercise commits the participants only to the joint action in effect before the first move. Further, except when the veto power is exercised:

Property (2) OBJECTIVE ACHIEVEMENT. The procedure insures that the participant's objective will be achieved after a finite number of steps;

Property (3) PRE-INDETERMINANCY. The procedure allows each participant to insure that for any number of initial steps, the joint proposals which may be reached cannot be determined uniquely by the other participant prior to these steps;

Property (4) GUARANTEED IMPROVEMENT. The procedure insures that on any move the joint proposal reached will not be less preferred by any participant to the joint proposal reached on the previous move, and will be preferred by at least one participant;

Property (5) LIMITED COMMITMENT. On any move the procedure allows each participant to limit the extent of change in the joint proposal (action) reached on the previous move to which he is willing to agree (commit himself).

Nguyen Be and his mule made it to Ban Cang, a village a few miles south of Dien Bien Phu, just before sunset. There he stayed the night in the hut of his cousin, Ban Pang, and his cousin's wife, a younger woman not pleased by the visit. The following morning the old man set out early again for the next village, Bam Pom Lot. He entered this village before noon and spent the better part of the afternoon hours smoking with the older villagers. Two days later Nguyen Be spent the afternoon and evening at a Buddhist pagoda outside the village of Muong Leo, north of the foot of Phon Sam Sao, one of the tallest mountains on the border with Laos.

It took Nguyen Be two days to make his way on a path that wound along the side of Phom Sam Sao to a ridge overlooking the opposite slope of the mountain. Nguyen Be knew of the path because as a boy he once had travelled south this way with his father and two uncles. To find it one had to keep on the road until it narrowed to a path at the foot of the mountain and from there always to keep in view a large fistlike rock just to the left of the ridge. Once the rock was attained, the path over the ridge was to be found between two ancient elms standing like portals to the other side of the mountain, which looked down on the lush forests of Laos and the river Het.

This part of the journey was most difficult for Nguyen Be. For most of the journey the path along the mountain slope was too narrow for the mule-cart. The old man had to move stones and hack at underbrush to move advance. More than once the mule balked, refused to budge, sat down and turned his head away. When the mule did this the old man cursed and threatened him with a stick, and once, in a fit of rage, he bit the mule on the ear. In his own time the mule heeded the old man's words, raised first one haunch and then the other, and dragged the wagon a few feet further, turning with indifferent eyes whenever the large wooden wheels became lodged between stones or whenever the whole cart spilled over on its side.

The two of them together slept away the hot afternoon under the shade of a cypress tree, and later, when night fell, the old man made a pillow of his sack of rice, covered himself with his blanket and slept on his side with his back against the mule's belly.

The next morning, before the fog in the valley below began rising from the ground, the lizards awoke them and they were on the move again. There was less undergrowth as they came nearer the fist-shaped rock, so their travel was easier now. Before the heat of the next afternoon was on them, Nguyen Be found the two ancient elms. He spent the afternoon resting beneath the elms, but he could not sleep. The crusty bark of the old trees reminded him of his father's face and of the skin on his father's arms, and he thought too of the stories his father told him about the tiger who came down out of the Burmese jungle and roamed the sides of this mountain until some villagers brought him a live pig and asked him to be their king; how when the Chinese invaded from the north the tiger filled the heavens with his thunder until the invaders went howling back to their own land; how one day a poor farmer found the tiger weeping at the foot of this every elm because his people were starving in the villages far to the south and the tiger felt helpless to travel there for fear of being killed along the way; and how after telling his tale of woe the tiger ceased weeping and devoured the poor farmer. In all his days Nguyen Be had never seen a tiger, but he always believed and even now thought he saw tiger eyes shining in the night. Not that he had any fear, though he knew it hid by day and killed men only at night when the victims were alone and too far from home to get any help. He had no fear of the tiger because he was an old man who knew his fate. He regretted only that he would die before he ever saw the tiger, and that this journey would be his last chance to be away from the villages where the tiger, because he felt remorse for eating the poor farmer, seldom showed himself again.

Nguyen Be carried these thoughts past the two ancient elms and onto the stony path leading to the ridge looking down the opposite side of the mountain. By sunset he and his mule had made their way to the top of the ridge where they found a grassy knoll to spend the night. Here he untied the mule from the cart and built a small fire to boil some rice. From here he could see the river Het as it wound like a snake around green hills and disappeared against a blue mountain farther to the south, and he watched as a small airplane, so high it was silent in the sky, disappeared from view even while one solitary bird, black and even smaller in the sky, glided in large circles above the summit of Phon Sam Sao until it got lost in the dusk. From here too he watched the Laoatian border patrol, two men in green suits steering a small craft in the river below, inch their way in and out of view around the hills, unaware, as they smoked their cigarettes, of the old man sitting cross-legged next to the glowing embers of his fire, or of the bird gliding between them and the sun that glared in the water before their eyes.

*   *   *

DOCUMENT NO. 7

Diary of Cat Mon, Member of the G464 Demolition Unit of the My Tho Province 415th Local Force Battalion

May 7, 1966: Tonight I can't go to sleep. I keep thinking of one thing and another. I'm lost in thought under the light of the lunar month, while all the others sleep peacefully. All day today I stayed in my hole clutching a carbine and looking across the canal toward the enemy post. Someday soon I know we will have to attack in the middle of the night. We are indifferent to the coming of spring.

I think now and then of Banh Anh, but whenever I do I fear I will never see her again. I saw what the Americans did with their bombs in the village of Cai Mon, and later in the day I heard bombs with my own ears. This spring how can we be happy when the Americans are still sowing so many sorrows and miseries, and when thousands of tons of bombs are falling on our villages, destroying and setting houses on fire, stripping the trees bare of leaves, forcing the people to wander from place to place. How can I be happy when I think of all this? The only thing we can do is transform our hatred into action to bring a spring of victory to the people.

Today we had the fourth day of our three-month training course. I must admit I was afraid when I handled the bangalore mine, and I will have to work to overcome my fear. And I confess that I felt envy for Vi Thanh, the battalion commander, whom I knew as a foolish schoolboy when I lived in Vinh Loc. But I dream now of the day the revolution will succeed and the Americans are drowned in the canals. I dream of uniting with our brothers in the north.

I must stop now because it is forbidden to keep a diary.

SAIGON (AP)—In the air war, U.S. fighter-bombers hit North Vietnam with more than 300 strikes on Monday for the fifth successive day. The U.S. Command said more than 330 strikes were flown.

The targets included the MIG base at Yen Bai, 30 miles northwest of Hanoi, where Air Force pilots reported several explosions, and the Thai Binh army barracks 37 miles southwest of Haiphong, where Navy pilots reported destroying 16 buildings.

Nearly 100 B52s attacked targets around the North Vietnamese port of Dong Hoi, 45 miles north of the demilitarized zone, and around the South Vietnamese cities of Saigon, Kontun, Quang Ngai, Da Nang, Hue, My Tho, and Quang Tri.

The U.S. Command said their targets were supply caches, troop positions and staging areas.

Associated Press correspondent Holger Jensen reported from the front north of Saigon that in five days communist forces have occupied at least seven hamlets and one village along an eight-mile stretch of Highway 13.

North Vietnamese and Viet Cong forces held on to a string of hamlets 14 to 22 miles north of Saigon today, and the South Vietnamese command acknowledged that its troops were making no effort to drive them out.

Nguyen Be hoped to meet up with the border patrol, for once down the southern slope of Phon Sam Sao he no longer knew the way. He began his descent, knowing only that he was to reenter Vietnam at the Barthelemy Pass near the village of Muong Sen about a hundred miles to the south. By evening he was down off the mountain and was boiling rice on a small fire on the banks of the river Het.

Until night fell, bringing with it a cover of clouds that enshrouded him in total dark, he sat next to the river, watching as the swifter current in the center carried drifting reeds away. He awoke once in the middle of the night, frightened by the sound of lizards, and a chill ran through him when he saw that the fire had dwindled to two glowing coals.

The next morning he tied his mule to a reed and tried passage along the riverbank on foot. In a few minutes he found himself in mud and tangled vines. The river, which from above looked like a shiny snake with its head buried in the earth, now was invisible a few feet from its own shore. He went back to the fireside, untied the mule, and sat down to smoke. He decided to wait for someone to show the way.

Two days later in the middle of Nguyen Be's afternoon nap a youth fishing on the stream drifted by on a raft made of wood and reeds. They would not have seen each other had a fly not bitten the mule's ear, causing a quiver to go through the mule's stomach that made the old man open one eye in time for him to see the boy and his raft disappear around the bend in the river. He called out to the boy and in a few moments heard him paddling toward him against the stream.

The boy was from the village of Ban Bong downstream. He could take the old man and his cart there, but not the mule. There the old man could make contact with the border patrol, who hid their boat near the village and spent nights, even whole days, with the wife of a young fisherman who one day left her and never returned. Then, if he was lucky, the old man could persuade the boy's uncle to come back for the mule on a raft big enough to hold them all.

Three days later Nguyen Be was walking along National Highway Seven just outside the village of Muong Sen with his mule and cart. He had reentered Vietnam at the Barthelemy Pass, eyed there with suspicion by the border patrol. He would have to make two more stops along the way, one at the village of Khe Bo where the boy's uncle had a cousin, and another at Xom Long Moc, where one of the Laotian border patrolmen had a brother.

When he finally reached the outskirts of Muong Sen, Nguyen Be sat down on a stone and massaged his feet.

*   *   *   *

The Veto-Incremax Procedure:
POTENTIAL FOR VIETNAM CONFLICT RESOLUTION

There are several possible Veto-Incremax procedures. (Incremax is an abbreviation for incremental maximization, and involves a maximization process taken over each of a series of small steps.) Each has the following appealing features:

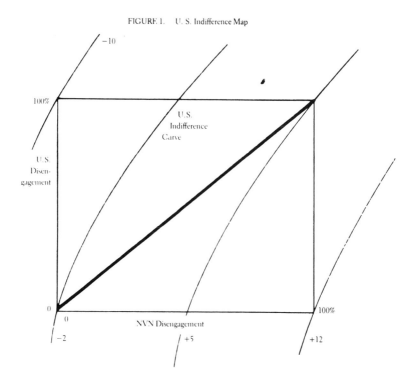

FIGURE 1.   U. S. Indifference Map

DOCUMENT NO. 11

Activities of the PRP Youth Group Chapter

Meeting of January 14, 1966 to Criticize the Party Chapter

1. The Party Chapter did not behave in an exemplary manner. For example, the Party Chapter members did not show up at the fortified trenches right away even when their subordinates had all taken up position there.

2. The Party Chapter members are still quick tempered.

3. Their working method is still unclear.

4. They do not observe discipline well.

5. They fail to show a good sense of unity; for example, they do not give much assistance to their subordinates.

6. Their assistance to the PRP Youth Group was superficial.

7. They do not pay much attention to the opinions of their subordinates. They are negligent in their work and very overbearing toward their subordinates.

Emulation

1. An emulation campaign should be launched during the training course. The Party members, cadres, and fighters will all have to take part in it with enthusiasm.

2. Good results should be obtained. Over eighty percent of the requirements should be fulfilled.

3. In order to make sure that all 100 percent of the unit participate in the training course, the Party Chapter has to be strict about enforcing disease-prevention measures, making the men observe hygienic practices and feeding them well.

4. The unit members should maintain unity and help each other.

5. Everyone, from the cadres down to the fighters, should observe the regulations concerning the training period.

6. Everyone should make an effort to save time and develop their initiative.

7. Serving the unit: When the subordinates make a request, the cadres should immediately act on it to help these subordinates.

Nguyen Be arrived at the house of San Kim, his nephew, six weeks after leaving Dien Bien Phu. As he and his mule approached the hamlet outside the village of Thuong Duc, word of his arrival spread even to the workers in the fields, and the people gathered in the hamlet to welcome him. They had many questions for him. They asked him if he knew their relatives in the north and how things in general went there. They asked if he had seen any fighting along the way, and he said no. They asked him to carry gifts to relatives in the south, and he made a careful list of all the villages along the way in which he, in exchange for food and a place to sleep, would deliver tidings, a letter, a gift.

That evening he and some of the villagers gathered around a fire in the center of the village. One of the older boys asked Nguyen Be if he had seen any Americans along the road. Nguyen Be said no, he had not stayed on the roads but had travelled the trails from village to village. Then they told the old man stories about the Americans, stories that chilled him to the bone. Secretly he was well-pleased with the stories. They gave him the same feelings he had when, as a boy, he sat quietly on the edge of the circle of men smoking around the village fire, listening late into the night as they told tales of days gone by, until he, giving up the struggle to stay awake, curled up in his father's lap and fell asleep.

Nguyen Be worked in the fields with his nephew San Kim for the next three days before moving on. On the evening of the third day he rearranged his provisions on the mulecart, refilled his white sack with new rice and placed a fresh bagful of carrots next to the small gifts he was carrying for the other villagers. He would have liked one thing more—a bagful of oats for his mule. He knew he would have to pass through the Kontum Plateau, and he knew the mule would have less to eat on high ground.

That night San Kim took him to a man with oats to spare. The man lived alone on the outskirts of the village, and when he spoke at all cursed the heat, the demon that had given him a sore back, and the Americans. He was known to be the hardest worker in the village and because he lived alone a man of wealth. Though he was known to give money to the poorest villagers, he was also the shrewdest businessman in the district.

The man, whose name was Buon Duc, bowed when he was introduced to Nguyen Be. "Respected sir," he said, "I understand you are on a long journey. I wish you good fortune and offer my assistance if I may serve."

"I have a simple need," Nguyen Be replied. "I need a bagful or two of oats for my mule, but I fear I have little to offer but a few piastres."

"Too few are seldom enough," the man of business said. "Though I want little more than to see you satisfied on your way, I cannot give away my goods, and to do so would be humiliating to you."

"I ask no favors. I will pay what I can, or I will be on my way."

"It goes without saying."

"What do you ask, then, for one bag?"

"Twenty piastres."

"Impossible, given my situation."

"But fair, given mine."

"At that I'd take a loss. I have an aunt in a village just north of here. She is old and destitute. For twelve I could hire a man to take the oats to her."

"I'd be a fool then to offer you more," Nguyen Be replied, "and thereby take food from your poor aunt's mouth."

"For eighteen I could endure the loss. Then both you and she would have oats."

"Eighteen is unthinkable."

"What then would you consider endurable, given my situation?"

"I would offer you twelve."

"And feel no remorse for the death of my aunt?"

"For her death, no. Besides, you say she is old now. Therefore she deserves to die."

"A hard logic, especially from one who is no boy."

"But I do not ask the oats for myself. They are for my poor mule, who is but a child. Therefore I will repeat my offer of twelve."

"And I, out of pity for you but with still more pity for my dying aunt, reluctantly accept."

"I'll take two bags at that price, because once I give you my piastres for your oats my heart will travel lighter."

The two men bowed to each other and Nguyen Be paid Buon Duc. In his purse he had only six piastres left, but he now had gifts to bear and friends along the way. His mule nosed the bags of oats on the ground until Buon Doc lifted them into the cart.

"I have one more bag of oats remaining. I might as well throw them in with the rest," said Buon Duc.

"I can give you three piastres, no more," said Nguyen Be.

"For ten I would let you have them, but my aunt would never forgive me."

"I know you'll be off to her place as soon as I depart," the old man said with a wink. "Good speed to you."

"And to you, respected sir. Remember me if you should come back this way and need more oats."

The next morning Nguyen Be looked down the road before him with a sigh. His back was sore from sleeping on a bed too soft, and his heart seemed as unwilling as his feet to go. Finally he embraced Sao Kim and his wife and said farewell. In the east the sun was just beginning to show itself over the rim of a ricefield, but already workers were bending over the earth. His mule sneezed, sending the flies circling his head away. The flies disappeared for a moment, but by the time Nguyen Be once more told San Kim not to weep for his going, the flies had returned to his circle the mule's impatient ears.

DOCUMENT NO. 21

Excerpts From "Cultural Classes"

Translator's Note: following are a few samples of the problems in arithmetic that the Demolition Unit members studied in the cultural classes. The notebook in which these problems are found belongs to Thanh Liem.

September 13

Problem: A unit is given 15 boxes of explosives, each box weighing 24.50 Kgs, to make 150 bangalores. How much does each bangalore weigh?

Problem: A rectangle plot of land measure 45 m long and 35 m wide. Two roads, each 1.50 m in width, are built one along the length of the land and the other along the width of the land. What is the remaining surface area of the plot of land?

Problem: A comrade goes on mission, going from his house to the unit. It takes him 6 hours to reach the unit on foot, and he covers 4.50 km in each hour. On his return trip home, he is in a hurry and borrows a bicycle, and it takes him only 2 hours to arrive at his house. How many kilometers did he cover by bicycle in one hour?

DOCUMENT NO. 16

Daily Time Schedule of the 2nd Squad
The Liberation Armed Forces of South Vietnam

Letter box: 7809m
2nd Squad

SCHEDULE

Morning

4:45 AM	Getting up
From 4:45 AM to 4:50 AM	Gathering for morning roll call
From 4:50 AM to 5:00 AM	Calisthenics
From 5:00 AM to 5:20 AM	Personal hygiene
From 5:20 AM to 5:40 AM	Breakfast (unless something happens)
From 5:40 AM to 7:20 AM	Getting ready for combat
From 7:20 AM to 11:30 AM	Studying and performing tasks
From 11:30 AM to 1:15 PM	Rest

Afternoon

From 1:15 PM to 1:30 PM	Getting up; getting ready to study
From 1:30 PM to 4:30 PM	Studying and performing tasks
From 4:30 PM to 5:10 PM	Review and cleaning weapons
From 5:10 PM to 6:00 PM	Bath and dinner
From 6:00 PM to 6:30 PM	3-man cell and squad activities
From 6:30 PM to 7:00 PM	Leisure time
From 7:00 PM to 8:30 PM	General activities and study
From 8:30 PM to 9:00 PM	Roll call, putting out all fires, going to bed

SLOGAN:

"VIGILANCE AND OBSERVATION OF DISCIPLINE AND
REGULATIONS ARE PART OF THE RESPONSIBILITY OF
THE TROOPS."

Since the first two stops Nguyen Be had to make were in the villages south of Thuong Duc along National Highway Fourteen, he decided to abandon the pathways and trails off the main road.

Just outside of the village of Kaduat Stoy he heard a loud roar on the road ahead of him. Leading his mule off the center of the road he continued forward, scanning the blue sky for signs of rain. As the roar came closer a nervous fright went through him, and he began looking in vain for escape. A young boy frantically pedalling a bicycle appeared over a rise in the road and shot past, waving his arms at the old man. A moment later an amtrack with a minesweeping brush turning before it appeared over the horizon. It was followed by a long column of trucks, three heavy tanks, and many armored cars.

Bewildered, Nguyen Be stopped by the roadside and tried to duck himself and his mulecart into high weeds. But it was too late. The trucks, as they turned down the road toward him, had seen him with their eyes. He stood still a moment, frozen in awe of the metallic dragon rolling toward him. As the amtrack came closer, the roar deafened him and his awe turned to terror and fear.

He pulled his hat down over his eyes, lowered his head, grabbed the left ear of his mule, and walked forward, turning his body slightly away as the column approached. He measured his steps and kept on, not looking up at the stiff green forms sitting atop the trucks saying things to him in a strange tongue.

Then, as suddenly as it had come on him, the dragon diminished behind, leaving him covered with the foul smell of diesel and dust. The memory of its roar stayed until he breathed clean air again, then even the memory disappeared against the sharp cry of birds flitting away over the weeds. Once more he was alone with his mule and cart on the road, and when he was sure of this he stopped to sit and have a smoke.

But there was no peace in this pause. Even when the column was so far away Nguyen Be could hear nothing but the wind blowing over the grass and the frantic buzz of insects, the hint of a heavy quaking seemed to pass like waves through his bones. His heart too was beating wildly like a bird's, though all the birds by now had gone into hiding. Bewildered, the old man bent down and put an ear to the ground. There he heard a rumble like that of a train passing in the night.

He roused his mule and started down the highway, looking in vain for a path off the main road. When he got fifty meters from his starting place, another sound, small and swifter this time, came out of the highway in front of him, and before he could turn into the weeds, a jeep with two green men in it was flying toward him.

Nguyen Be had no time to hid his face. At first he saw only the round white eyes and square silver grin of the jeep itself. Then he saw the two men, the driver with his head lowered. The other was following him, as they approached each other, through the sights of a big gun. When they were upon each other the soldier with the gun drew his head back, and, lowering the gun as the jeep and mulecart met, smiled. In that flying moment their eyes met, paused in a crossed perplexity. They saw each other still after their passing apart.

In a moment the men and the jeep disappeared into the dust on the highway, but he heard it long after it passed out of view, groaning as it struggled up and around the steep inclines, a drunk man angry at the work the sky had imposed on him.

DOCUMENT NO. 31

Daily Review of Morale and Resolutions
by a Squad Member*

May 14
Dissatisfaction with superiors. When the collectivity "expressed their opinion" [VC expression for "criticism"] I did not realize that their criticism was correct. Later on, I criticized myself and realized that the criticism of the collectivity was correct.

I promise to overcome my error.

May 28
Good morale, as shown in my performance of various tasks.

I promise to develop this good point.

May 30
Good morale. I performed my tasks well; for example, I took good care of the money that Comrade Buon Duc forwarded to the unit.

I promise to develop this good point.

June 6

Good morale and firm ideological stand. Maintenance of unity. Good performance of tasks. I hid my personal effects well. I observed discipline and did not commit any violations of discipline. I economized and took good care of equipment. Study: I read books on my own.

I promise to develop these good points.

June 7

Morale: my mind was at ease, and my ideological stand did not waver. I maintained unity, performed my tasks well, and observed the formation of the unit in the bivouacking area. I observed discipline; for example, I was careful when I hung my clothes out to dry. I economized and took good care of equipment—I did not damage anything. Study: I read books on my own.

I promise to develop these good points.

June 8

Morale: no deteriorating changes. I maintained unity and did not have conflicts with anyone. Performance of tasks: I pulled a sampan ashore and washed it. Observation of discipline: I overslept. I economized and took good care of equipment. Study: I studied on my own.

I promise to develop these good points.

June 9

Good morale: no bad changes. I maintained unity and did not have conflicts with any comrades. Performance of tasks: I pulled a sampan ashore and washed it clean of mud. I observed discipline and did not commit any violations. I economized and took good care of equipment—I did not damage anything. Study: I studied on my own.

I promise to develop these good points.

June 10

Good morale: no bad changes. I maintained unity within my cell as well as in my relationship with the other cells; I did not have conflicts with anyone. I performed my tasks zealously: for example, I scooped up soil and poured it in the vegetable patches to grow vegetables. I observed discipline and did not commit any violations. I economized and took good care of equipment. Study: I studied on my own.

I promise to develop these good points.

* *A notebook in the handwriting of Cat Mon.*

The Veto-Incremax Procedure:
POTENTIAL FOR VIETNAM CONFLICT RESOLUTION

It should be stressed at this point that the numbers associated with these indifference curves are not basic to the analysis which follows. Any other set of numbers which orders the indifference curves of the U.S. in the same way is just as relevant. We use the numbers of Figure 1 simply because they have been already used in Table 1.

In a similar manner we construct in Figure 2 the indifference curves for North Vietnam, who may be taken to be Player 2. These curves are dashed in order to distinguish them from those for the U.S.

FIGURE 2. NVN Indifference Map

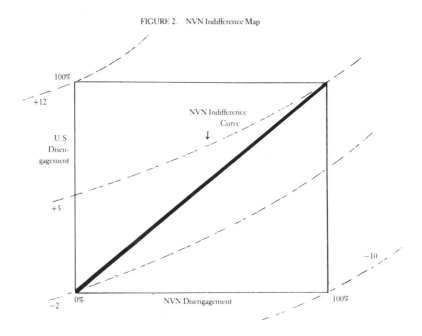

In Figure 3 we superimpose those indifference curves of the two sets which are relevant for the analysis to ensue. Now, to repeat, the problem is how to go from the lower left-hand corner of Figure 3, which corresponds to 0% disengagement by each of the parties, and which lies on each one's indifference curve of −2, to the point at the upper right-hand corner of the box, which corresponds to 100% disengagement by each party and the indifference curves of +5.

DOCUMENT NO. 33

Personal Data

1. Real Name: Cat Mon. Alias: Cai Tho.
2. DOB: 1943
3. Date of recruitment: July 20, 1963.
4. Rank: Assistant Squad Leader (assigned October 5, 1965). Function: Squad Leader (assigned December 10, 1966).
5. Name of person signing orders: Muoi Quoc.
6. POB: Phuoc Thanh Village, Chau Thanh District, My Tho Province. Residence: Phuoc Thanh Village, Chau Thanh District, My Tho Province.
7. Ethnic origin: Vietnamese.
8. Political affiliation: none.
9. Education: third year of Elementary School.
10. Classification: Poor Farmer — Family: Poor Farmer; myself: Poor Farmer.
11. Profession: farmer.
12. Date of admission into PRP Youth Group: April 13, 1965. Date of admission into Party: N/A. (Probationary: N/A Official: N/A).
13. Names of two persons making introduction for Party membership: N/A.
14. Highest Party function: none.
15. Health: B classification.
16. Wounds: wounded once in right thigh.
17. Father's name: Cat Thoi (living). Mother's name: Tran Thi Dang (living). Parent's residence: Phuoc Thanh Village, Chau Thanh District, My Tho Province.
18. Relatives: My older brother, Le Van Nhieu, is working for the Revolution in Phuoc Thanh Village. A cousin of mine is serving in the Chau Thanh District Demolition Unit. Ban Pang, my wife's uncle, regrouped to the North. My wife's two younger brothers are serving in the Chau Thanh District Local Force. Be Ba, a cousin of mine, is serving in Eastern Nam Bo.
19. Training courses attended: a 20-day military training course organized by the province, and a 10-day political training course organized by the province.
20. Commendations: I was awarded a commendation paper once.
21. Disciplinary measures: I have never been disciplined.

For the next two lunar months Nguyen Be, taking trails from village to village, made his way through the Central Highlands. For a good part of the voyage he found passage for himself and his mule and cart with an old riverman who had spent years at sea but now enjoyed nothing more than to steer his small sampan through the small rivers that wound their crooked circular courses around the feet of mountains before joining another tributary that emptied into still another stream going south.

Through all his journeys with the riverman Nguyen Be never knew where he was. Many times he tried to gauge his course by the sun and stars, and many times he was sure he was heading north rather than south. But each time the old riverman, flashing a toothless smile, assured him that the water knew the most effortless path. Nguyen Be believed the old man. They smoked together many times each day and night. And each day they caught a few fish and boiled their rice with the shoots of bamboo and leaves of other plants the old riverman gathered along the way.

And they talked late into the night. The old riverman told him tales about the sea, of his exploits as a harpooner on a Japanese whaling ship and of his conquests of beautiful women in all the ports of the East. He talked of death and of seeing Uncle Ho in a village in the north. Nguyen Be told him he had seen Americans, and in a whisper about the three sisters he used to meet together in the fields just a few years ago.

Sometimes the stories they told each other made him tremble. One night Nguyen Be asked the old riverman if he had ever seen a tiger in the highlands. "Just once," the riverman replied. "But at night I heard him many times." Not roaring, he said, as one would expect a tiger to do, but threshing restlessly in the brush along the riverside and at times growling a low growl like the moan of sorrow an old man feels when his wife has died. He saw the tiger once drinking water from the River Rue, and it looked tired and old. It was startled by a single American plane streaking overhead, and he never saw it again.

Finally, after their many nights and days together, the two old men parted at the village of Doc Bon. From here, the old riverman said, it would be easy to find river passage or to go on foot from village to village until Nguyen Be reached his brother's home in the south. On the morning of their last day together they kneeled with a Buddhist monk at the pagoda and then slept the afternoon away. The night before they parted they said little while they smoked, and the next morning Nguyen Be turned away to resume his own journey on foot, as the old riverman, poling his sampan against the current, passed from view around a bend in the river.

*　　　　*　　　　*　　　　*

Diary of the Unit Platoon Leader

May 26, 1966

One squad composed of 13 comrades will be needed in the target area.

The Following Comrades Will Take Part in the Attack

—Hong, Squad Leader:
>> handling 1 Thompson, to cover the other comrades.

—Hiep, Squad Leader:
>> handling 1 FTC-6 (apparently a type of mine). This mine should be planted secretly and will be the first one to be triggered.

—Thoai, Assistant Squad Leader:
>> handling 1 FTC-6, to attack the embankment.

—Kiet, Assistant Squad Leader:
>> handling 1 Thompson, to provide cover for the other comrades.

—Ba, Assistant Squad Leader:
>> handling 1 HTT4, to attack the second block-house (HTT4 is apparently another kind of mine).

—Muoi, Assistant Squad Leader:
>> handling 1 FTC-6 to attack the Van Sap bridge.

—Minh, Cell Leader:
>> handling 1 FTC-6, to assist in the attack on the Van Sap bridge.

Replacements in Case any Comrades Sacrifice Their Lives During Combat
>—Tam will be the leader during the attack; if he is killed, comrade Phuoc will take his place and act as commander.
>—Phuoc will be the deputy leader during the attack; if he is killed, comrade Hong will replace him.
>—If comrade Hong is killed, comrade Hiep will replace him.

Assignment of tasks to each Comrade
> a.—Hiep, handling one FT, will be the first to explode his mine. He has the mission of planting his mine secretly at the first block-house and of exploding it when an order to that effect is issued.
> —Ba, handling one HT, will be the second one to explode his

mine. After the first mine explodes, he has the task of exploding his HT mine to destroy what is left of the first blockhouse.

—Ngon, handling one FT, will keep it in reserve in order to reinforce the first cell when necessary.

b. —Manh, handling one FT, will be the third one to explode his mine. He has the task of attacking the barracks housing enemy troops.

—Hai, handling one HT, will be the fourth one to explode his mine. He has the task of destroying the barracks housing enemy troops.

—Son, handling one FT, will keep it in reserve in order to reinforce the second cell when necessary.

—Phuoc has the special task of cutting the fence to enable Hien to plant his mine secretly and to enable the assault group to move in.

—Muoi and Viet, handling two FT, have the task of destroying the bridge. Whenever the Command Staff issues an order to this effect, they will have to perform their task quickly.

c. —Hong and Kiet, handling one Thompson each, have the task of shooting the sentinel. If the mine that is planted secretly is detected, they should shoot the sentinel immediately.

—After the first and second mines explode, these two comrades should fire fiercely into the enemy barracks, and at the same time they should provide cover for comrades Manh and Hai, handling the third and fourth mines, to enable them to achieve their task of attacking the central target.

—Comrade Ho has the task of following the attacking point into combat and bandaging the wounded, if there are any.

The Veto-Incremax Procedure:
POTENTIAL FOR VIETNAM CONFLICT RESOLUTION

We now envisage a series of moves in a step-by-step improvement process for each party. On each move, each party is to make a proposal for a joint action. These proposals are, however, to be subject to the following rules:

RULE 1: In making any proposal for a joint action, each player shall not consider a joint action which would yield any participant an outcome less preferred than the joint proposal reached in the preceding move. On move 1 this rule means that each participant's proposal for a joint action must lie within or on the boundary of that shaded area defined within the larger box by the pair of indifference curves which course through the initial position of 0%-0% disengagement.

RULE 2: On each move no player can propose a joint action which lies outside the commitment set. In Figure 1 the commitment set for the first move is the small, heavily shaded box which centers around the 0%-0% point. This commitment set is obtained by first identifying the maximum change along both the vertical and horizontal which each participant is willing to allow on that move, and then by taking the least of these maximums first along the vertical and then along the horizontal. Recall that change along the vertical represents percentage change in U.S. disengagement and that change along the horizontal represents percentage change in NVN disengagement.

RULE 3: If on any move the proposed joint actions of the participants are not identical, the participants shall adopt as a compromise proposal that joint action defined by the mid-point of the straight line connecting the proposed joint actions of the two participants. In Figure 3, the point P^1 is the midpoint of the straight line connecting N^1 and U^1, the proposed joint actions of NVN and U.S., respectively. Thus, P^1 represents a compromise or joint proposal.

FIGURE 3. The Determination of the Joint Proposal of the First Move

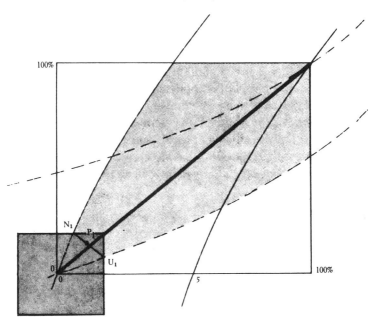

RULE 4: On any move, no player can propose a joint action which is more preferred by him to the 100% joint disengagement action. By this rule we define a restricted improvement set. This set on any move is bounded by the indifference curves of the two participants which pass through the 100%-100% disengagement point and those which pass through the joint proposal reached on the previous move. In Figure 4, the restricted improvement set on the second move is thus P^1HJKP^1.

RULE 5: Once a move is reached where one player can propose a joint action whose outcome is not less preferred by him to the 100% joint disengagement point, the other player may choose as a final joint action any joint action which is not less preferred by the first to the 100% joint disengagement point.

It is evident that whenever Rule 5 is applicable, the objective can be immediately attained through a proposal of a joint action by the second player.

We have now illustrated a possible use of one type of veto-incremax procedure. There are at least several other types that can be constructed and examined for applicability. One would substitute for the split-the-difference principle in Rule 3 an alternating leader-follower principle. Another might substitute a weighted compromise principle where different rather than equal weights are assigned to joint actions proposed by the participants on any move. The commitment sets might be defined differently. And so forth. The reader is referred elsewhere for further discussion.

We conclude with the hope that we have now laid bare several procedures which can be examined and investigated in terms of their potential applicability to major conflict situations. It is not expected that these procedures may have direct application to all conflict situations, or even to a large fraction of such situations—or even to existing situations such as the Paris talks, the Middle East, or the urban confrontations in the United States. If however they do provide some assistance in mediating some important conflict, the effort that has gone into the development of game theory and these procedures will have been justified.

DOCUMENT NO. 36

List of Lost Equipment

Comrade Hong lost:	1 knapsack, 2 pairs of long pants (Main Force type), 1 (Main Force) shirt, 1 nylon hammock, 1 mosquito net, 1 blanket, 1 rice pouch.
Comrade Manh lost:	1 pouch, 2 pairs of (Main Force) long pants, 2 (Main Force) shirts, 1 black pajama top, 1 pair of shorts, 1 rice pouch, 1 radio, 1 mosquito net, 1 blanket.
Comrade Thoai lost:	1 pouch, 2 long-sleeved shirts (1 made of Popeline fabric and 1 made of Nylfranc fabric), 2 pairs of long pants (one (Main Force) pair of pants made of Popeline fabric, and one pair made of Fine fabric), 1 mosquito net, 1 blanket.
Comrage Ngon lost:	1 knapsack, 1 pair of (Main Force) long pants, 2 shirts (one long sleeved, and one (Main Force) type), 2 pairs of shorts, 1 mosquito net, 1 blanket, 1 nylon sheet (3 m), 1 pair of long pants (made of gray khaki).

May 5, 1967   For the Command Staff of the Demolition Section,
Ngo Van Xe

Six days after leaving the old riverman Nguyen Be entered Ben Cat, a marketplace town just north of Saigon. Since early in 1962 Ben Cat had been the focus of many military moves code-named "Operation Sunrise." But nothing much about the town had changed, except for the wire fence surrounding it and the large wooden watchtower rising just above the wild forests.

Nguyen Be and his mule were stopped on the outskirts of the town by an ARVN soldier who asked him to produce identification papers. When the old man said he had none, the soldier nosed around the belongings in the cart, and, with a gesture of indifference, waved him on. Passing the market, Nguyen Be saw the wooden tower and paused to marvel at it. He had never seen such a tower before in any of the other villages. It seemed so unusual to him that it forced him to laugh, and one of the farmers saw and laughed with him. In the market Nguyen Be saw many people, for it was still early in the morning.

He made his way to the house of the village chieftain, a small but solid wooden structure just to the left of the marketplace. The chieftain, a thin graying man well into his sixties, received him and in time discovered that his cousin was an old friend of Nguyen Be's ailing brother. The two men smoked together and talked away half the afternoon, and then Nguyen Be walked to the marketplace and smoked with the farmers there.

That evening the village chieftain invited Nguyen Be to have supper with him. Nguyen Be asked him which route to My Tho would be best, and the chieftain cautioned him to avoid the confusion of Saigon. "I have friends," he said, "in all the villages to the southeast—in Hien Liem, Gia Kiem, Lam Kuan, Phu My, and Dong Hoa. I could send a letter with you to these villages, and from Dong Hoa you can go across the canals to My Tho. But I have friends the other way too—in the villages of Trang Bang, Duc Hue, Tuyen Nhon, and Nhi My—and that is by far the shortest route, though you should beware of getting caught in the middle of a military sweep if you go the shortest route."

"I wish now I were a bird that could fly from here to My Tho," Nguyen Be said. "I've never seen the war yet, though I heard the battle when the French were driven out. I'm told everywhere I go that the war is a terrible thing. Yet whatever the danger, I must go the shortest route for I fear my brother may die before I arrive."

"Then it is settled. You will take the southwestern route, and I will have word sent of your arrival in the villages along the way."

"If we survive, my mule will thank you too," the old man smiled.

"I have arranged for you to stay the night in a hut outside Ben Cat. The hut is one of six set up to house young farmers in the region. It is in a thick part of the forest but you will be kept safe by the young men there."

"Safe even from stray tigers?"

"I assure you. The men there are warriors at heart."

"I will go."

"I ask one favor in return. I have a nephew in a hamlet outside of Nhi My who was wounded in the chest by a bomb. My aunt sent word that he is close to death. I want you to carry a burial coffin to her. Wood is very scarce in her district, and she is a widow and very poor."

Later the chieftain loaded the wooden box onto the mulecart and led Nguyen Be into the forest some distance from Ben Cat. As they came down a tangled trail they were greeted by a sentry, a boy no more than fifteen, who led them the rest of the way to a camp made of six straw-roofed huts held up by poles. Gathered around a central hut they found a dozen young men, all of them dressed in the plain clothes of peasant farmers. In the huts Nguyen Be saw piles of wooden crates covered by canvas cloth and bagfuls of rice shaped like horse collars for easy carrying. Stacked neatly outside the central hut were guns.

The young men greeted Nguyen Be, slid the coffin from the mulebox, untied the mule and tethered him to the central hut. Then some of them gathered wood in the forest and started a fire in the firepit of the central hut. When the stars appeared through the trees overhead, the young men gathered around Nguyen Be and the firepit, where one of them had prepared some tea for the others in the group. For a long time they listened to the old man tell stories about his youth and about his adventures along the way, and together they smoked and drank tea until there was no more left in the pot. In time the old man learned the names of all the young men in the camp, and the names of their villages. Only one—a solid youth named Vi Thanh, a leader—was from outside the Ben Cat district. He was, he said softly, from Vinh Loc, a village in the south.

After midnight Nguyen Be began making a bed of canvas sacks next to the firepit in the central hut, and like the coals of the fire the talk lost its glow and the men made their way to beds in the other huts. In a few minutes the camp was lost in the black silence of night, illumined only by the stars and glowing coals in the fire and pierced only by the mocking cries of lizards and nightbirds hidden in the dark.

Nguyen Be slept too deeply to dream that night, and his heavy sleep was the reason he failed to hear the warning whistle that roused the young men and sent them to their forest holes. The old man awoke to a whirring sound which, as it approached, sounded more like the rapid clapping of giant wings together. Suddenly the noise was overhead, sending a furious wind down on him. Then big white lights lit up the camp as if it were day, and he heard shouts everywhere in the night. Then the big bird seemed to slide away sideways into the sky and disappear.

Confused, Nguyen Be bolted up from his bed and ran to his mule, whose eyes looked like startled birds. He pulled the mule down and cowered beside him, feeling the warmth he gave off with the rapid rise and fall of his breathing. He wanted to call out but could see no one. He heard the sound of gunfire and heard shouting and thrashing in the bush. He grabbed his mule's ears and pulled his head down to the earth. Lights shone in on him from the forest, and he could see that he had been abandoned, that the guns were gone, the huts empty of wooden crates and bags of rice.

When he saw the first soldier walk toward him with a rifle raised in the firing position, he thought of his mule. The soldier told him to rise to his feet, and as he did he saw other soldiers, all of them in green, emerge from the darkness with their guns pointed at him. When he glanced to one side for a path of escape he saw more soldiers there, and though he could not see he felt them coming up from behind.

"Who are you?" a voice commanded out of the dark.

"I am Nguyen Be. I am an old man, and this is my mule."

"What were you doing here?" the voice commanded.

"I was sleeping here. I am on a long journey to see my dying brother, and I saw this camp and stayed here for the night." In the forest Nguyen Be saw the eyes of the twelve youths watching.

"Where are the others?" a different voice commanded.

"What do you mean?"

"Viet Cong."

"They are neither here nor there."

"We will kill you if you do not speak."

"Then I will speak. There were three men here with me—workers in a rubber plantation. They saw me on the road, took me in, fed me, gave me a bed to sleep on, and now they are gone. Need I speak on to save my life?"

"Only the truth will save your life. How many men were there?"

"Only three."

"Did they have guns?"

"None that I saw."

"Why did they go away?"

"The same reason I would have had I their youth. They were afraid and they ran. I would now run if I had legs, and fly if I had wings."

One of the men came forward toward him and began looking in the central hut. He found only the dying coals in the firepit, the teapot hanging over it, and the canvas bed Nguyen Be had made for himself. Then the soldier came toward him, eyed him up and down, and saw the mulecart. With his rifle he probed the bag of rice in the cart and then with one hand he opened the sack containing the small gifts destined for the chieftain's friends in villages along the way.

"Trinkets," the old man said.

"Then you can do without them," the soldier said as he took them from the cart. He then walked to the mule and with the barrel of his gun lifted the mule's left ear.

"Dare not touch my mule," the old man shouted. "The world would have nothing but shame for you if you dare touch my mule."

At this the mule lifted himself to his feet, his eyes still dancing with fear.

"And the shame is yours too for waking an old man from his sleep. You boys do not know what it is like to be old—to live in the fear that you some night will wake up to the nightmare of death. I live with that each night and waking day, and the shame is yours for violating my peace of mind. So be gone from here! Either take my life or take yourselves away!"

The circle of soldiers around Nguyen Be seemed to sink back, and for a moment no one spoke. Then another voice, the first, spoke out. "You say there were only three?"

"Only three—mere boys."

"And not armed?"

"Not soldiers—mere boys, peasant workers. That's what my eyes told me."

"Be gone, old man," said another in the dark. "And mind your head."

Within another hour the soldiers completed their search and called on their radio for the heliocopters to return. The soldiers left Nguyen Be in the central hut, reluctant to leave the stories he was telling them about his life as a riverboat captain on the Plain of Reeds and of his youthful life of sin and lust in the port of Haiphong. And before they left they persuaded the soldier with the gun to return his sack of trinkets.

When the hum of the second heliocopter disappeared into the sky, Nguyen Be, his legs weak now with fear, sat down and covered his head with a canvas sack. He sat silent for long moments, hearing nothing but the jungle and the frail beating of his own heart. He wanted to weep but could not. Above all, he wanted a place to hide—a small place away from the clearing in the forest.

Long before even a hint of dawn began to break over the trees, he left some water and an open bagful of oats by his mule and dragged the wooden coffin into the forest away from the camp. Spreading a canvas sack down on the planks, he then climbed in, closed the lid over his head, and slept a solid dreamless sleep.

By morning the twelve guerillas returned to the camp, and, with a watchful eye on the coffin not far from them on the forest floor, sat around the firepit of the central hut drinking tea.

*   *   *   *

Red Forces Control Areas Near Saigon

SAIGON (AP) — North Vietnamese and Viet Cong Forces held on to a string of hamlets 14 to 22 miles north of Saigon today, and the South Vietnamese command acknowledged that its troops were making no effort to drive them out.

In the air war, U.S. fighter-bombers hit North Vietnam with more than 300 strikes Monday for the fifth successive day. The U.S. Command said more than 330 strikes were flown.

The targets included the MIG base at Van Bai, 80 miles northwest of Hanoi, where Air Force pilots reported several explosions, and the Thai Binh army barracks 37 miles southwest of Haiphong, where Navy pilots reported destroying 16 buildings.

Nearly 100 U.S. B52s attacked targets around the North Vietnamese port of Dong Hoi, 45 miles north of the demilitarized zone, and around the South Vietnamese cities of Saigon, Kontum, Quang Ngai, Da Nang, Hue, My Tho, and Quang Tri.

The U.S. Command said their targets were supply caches, troop positions and staging areas.

Associated Press correspondent Holger Jensen reported from the front north of Saigon that in five days communist forces have occupied at least seven hamlets and one village along an eight-mile stretch of Highway 13.

BIOGRAPHY

(From the time I was seven years old to date)

From the time I was seven years old to the time I joined the army:

My parents were poor farmers. I attended the village school from the time I was seven years old till I was 13. I quit school then to help my family, doing miscellaneous chores. I worked as a servant from the time I was 16 years old till I was 19. I quit in that year—1962—to join the hamlet Self-defense militia. I disseminated leaflets, stood guard (five times) on the road while the civilian laborers destroyed the Strategic Hamlet, stood guard (seven times) while the laborers destroyed the road, stood guard (12 times) on the road while meetings were held, went along with the Chau Thanh District Local Force once to take over a post in Thanh Phu Village, Chau Thanh District, and one time I took up a blocking position [*nam an ngu*] while the Unit intercepted and attacked an enemy platoon led by Dung from the Thanh Phu post. The enemy platoon was going to Bo Xe Hamlet to conscript the people and force them to build Strategic Hamlets. The District Local Force with which I participated in the attack wiped this platoon off the map—this attack took place on July 20, 1963. After that I volunteered to join the Phuoc Thanh Village unit in Chau Thanh District. I was sent to the Province Engineering Unit, and was trained on the job by Thanh Thanh, Tu Hien and Sau Thai.

From the time I joined the unit to date:

While I was with the Province Engineering Unit I took part in an attack on a GMC truck at the end of November 1963. The truck was completely destroyed and eight enemy soldiers were killed. I also destroyed roads 13 times, destroyed bridges three times, exploded self-detonating mines (along with the Unit) to destroy five M113s. I myself personally destroyed one of these five M113s and afterward took refuge in a hold. On September 9, 1964 the Military Affairs transferred me to the G464 Generally speaking, my squad had taken part in every attack, destroying roads and so on.

July 14, 1967

Signed: Cat Mon.

Nguyen Be awoke the next morning and emerged from his wooden box when the sun, high overhead, had paused to glare down on him between the branches of two trees. As he approached the central hut, the men hardly noticed him, for they were listening intently to a stranger bringing news from My Tho. The stranger's name was Giong Tram. "The Americans came and went from My Tho," said Giong Tram, "and the fight led to the capture of many documents from a certain Cat Mon when dogs led the Americans to the hole he was hiding in."

"Did the dogs kill him?"

"He found another hole and escaped into the trees."

"Do you have any word," Nguyen Be asked Giong Tram, "of the well-being of a certain Hong Be, an aging farmer and orchard-keeper who lives near My Tho?"

"I know of one such man," Giong replied, "who lives on the southern road to the town across from the grain mill."

"That is the place."

"His wife took two of us in as sons one night when the Americans were looking for us. He was ill at the time, and said he was waiting for his brother from the north."

"I am the one," Nguyen Be said.

"He knew you were on the way. When I left him he looked as content as a sleeping child."

Himself now content, Nguyen Be spent another night at the camp talking with the men around the firepit of the central hut. The following morning the young men returned to their work, some to the rubber plantation, others to the farms. Nguyen Be, stroking the mule's ears while feeding him a carrot, said farewell to them all.

Two days later at sunset the old man arrived at a place where the Song Vam Co Tay River swelled into a small lake. On the other side of the river lay the village of Tuyen Nhon. Just south of there was Nhi My and one day's journey from Nhi My was My Tho.

This evening he would not search for passage across the river. There would be time for that in the morning. There would be time for him to be with his brother, for he probably never would return to the north. This evening he would content himself to watch the sun, a bright sphere touching the water's edge, sink into the water. He was also content to do without his bowl of rice. This evening he would sit and smoke.

While he smoked a solitary bird circled in the dusk high above. In the swift center of the stream a silent swan softly drifted down. Near shore reeds danced in rhythm with the water's grayest undulations.

THE CAT-HATER

Willy sat stone-still on a broken step at the back of the mess, zeroing in along the broomstick on the cat as it rummaged among the trashcans under the elm. Again the cat did not show itself, and again Willy had lifted the broom to his shoulder, lined up the imagined cat in his sights, and fired again and again. As his arms grew weary, he glimpsed the cat's shiny fur against one of the cans. He squeezed the trigger carefully, expecting the jolt of a recoil in his shoulder. "I'll get that black motherfucker yet," he hissed. And then the cat was gone, leaving behind only the noise of empty tin cans.

As long as he could remember he hated cats. "Some things must be inborn," he told the cook, "and this is one of them. Cats are sneaky, and you can't trust them. You can tell from their eyes. They have evil eyes—try to hypnotize you. You should never look in their eyes. And they're dirty and lazy. They eat garbage like rats and sleep all day. They never work or do anything. They're not like a dog, or a canary that at least sings for you. They sit looking down at you. They're only awake at night when they're sneaking around, and their shit stinks worse than anything. Cats are the dirtiest things in the world."

Most of the men didn't mind his talk, because even while he stood behind the huge potful of soup Willy complained about the food he scooped out to the men every afternoon and evening with a big wooden spoon. They could be sure he was looking out for them. "If there's been one fly in the soup," he announced every week, "you can be sure I won't let you have it. And you can be sure I'm keeping an eye out for you in that kitchen." All he asked in return was a little thanks. "Once in a while you should say it," he told them more than once a week.

So every day a few of the men said, "Thanks, William," and the others in line smiled with a nod and moved on. His real name was Willy but William was the name that stuck. In time he didn't answer the soldiers who called him Willy, and within a month he made it plain they wouldn't get a full serving of soup until they changed their ways.

So in time they changed their ways. They called him William until his old name got lost in the past, and they listened when he told them about cats, especially the big black one he swore he would get. He convinced most of them—cats were sneaky, lazy, evil-eyed and dirty—and no one dared to speak to him carelessly about cats. They laughed it off. So at first they dismissed it as easily as they forgot him after passing him in the soup line. He was one of those soldiers who didn't fight, who never drank, played poker, or went to the whorehouses in Saigon. He was a private, never imagined himself any higher up. "He a nigger like us," Lincoln Jones, a big black from Chicago, remarked in a whisper to another black in the soupline. "Willy gonna spend the rest of his life behind a potful of soup, and he be a grateful nigger too."

Well, thought Willy, it was better to spend the rest of your life here than back home. At least here you knew where you stood. Back home was a jungle. His father, a short lean-faced man who was losing his hair and who still spoke Italian when he was happy, tried to escape from New York City to Detroit. In New York one of the neighbor ladies got raped right outside the grocery they rented. After his father was held up a third time, he wrote the uncle in Detroit, and within six months and another robbery, they were on their way.

The uncle showed them a corner store off the busy streets with a two-bedroom apartment above the store. Willy's room remained bare for almost six months until his father bought him a rug, chest of drawers and floor lamp. The business was so good he talked his father into letting him quit school so he could help full-time.

He had big ideas then. He would buy the store someday, and he would buy a house for his mother close to the store. Every morning he took a dust-rag to the shelves and straightened the rows of cans and boxes. Within a year there was not enough work, so his father told him to get an afternoon job. If they could save two thousand dollars they could talk the owner into a mortgage, and they would be better off.

So he went to work nights in an east side restaurant owned by the uncle's friend. "We need a worker," the boss told him as he sized the boy up. "But you got to look clean—you got to get a haircut and wear a white shirt."

He hated his job after only two weeks. "They're pigs in that place," he told his mother. "There's garbage everywhere." The chef told Willy he was his best man in the kitchen. Every night the kitchen crew made way for Willy to put the place in order. He began in one corner, making it as tidy as the perfect rows of cans and boxes he left piled in his father's grocery every morning. But by midnight the busboys left Willy a heap of garbage and trays he could not face, so he turned his back on it all just before walking to the bus stop for his long ride home through the sleeping city streets. "They're pigs," he thought.

Willy cursed even the chef. Willy asked him once what to do with some scraps of meat. "Throw them in the garbage and put them in back with the rest of the trash," the chef said. "The niggers will be by later tonight and lick it all up." Everyone but Willy laughed at this, even the old gray-haired black who had washed dishes for twenty years.

"Why don't you put them in the soup?" Willy asked.

"Because then the niggers would have to work for a living," the chef said. And everyone laughed, even Willy this time.

But it was a waste and when no one was looking Willy stuffed the scraps of meat into a bag and took them home. Willy knew his father's words, words inherited from a long line of fathers who had scraped a living by hand out of the ground: "If you want to eat, you have to work."

By the end of the first year Willy had saved enough for a mortgage loan, but his father told him that if he worked another year they could almost buy the store. Midway through the second year someone broke into the store. It happened on one of those hot August nights when the heat is so thick in old upstairs flats that the air feels like old dust. All three were half-asleep when they heard the clatter at the back of the store, and all three froze when they heard the footsteps on the wood below.

"Willy," his father whispered through the door. "Willy, you hear them? Be quiet, Willy, and don't move. Maybe they will go away."

He lay naked on the bed, numb with fear. What if they come up here, he wondered. What can we do if they come up here? There was no money in the store. He knew that his father kept only a few bills there, that he hid the rest somewhere. He waited, straining to hear noises that never came again. "A gun," he said to himself. "I wish I had a gun. Then they would leave us alone."

The idea glowed in his mind during the minutes he lay in the bed waiting in a frozen rage of shame and impotence. No, he thought, I'd go after them. They would hear me coming—but I'd go after them.

When they had gone he felt his legs go weak. He called the police before going downstairs, his mother in tears pleading for them to wait until the police arrived. The few dollars his father left in the register were gone, the lock on the back door broken, and that was all. All, that is, except for the fear that entered their home that night like a bodiless shadow, a fear they had left behind in New York when he was too young to know it the way his mother and father did.

"I'm going to buy a gun," he told his father.

"No," his father said. "No, it's worse that way. Then they can kill you."

"If they want to kill us what can we do without a gun?"

"They won't kill us if we have no gun. You must promise me you will not get a gun. I will not have a gun in my house. A gun gives them a right to kill us, and if they come you should give everything to them."

At the end of the week Willy stopped at a pawnshop and for six dollars bought a small pistol which he hid in an old shoe. And two months later he returned from work to find all the lights on. His mother's eyes were big with fear. "They robbed us," she said. "They wore black socks over their faces with slits for the eyes and they came upstairs," and when his father said he had only what was in the register downstairs they fired right past his head. And they took five hundred dollars his father kept in the old radio.

His father looked weary and small that night, even when he winked at Willy and told him he had a secret for him. There were four thousand dollars in the old Bible. He kept it there just in case the banks went broke, the way they did during the Depression, and Willy now should know.

That night Willy put his pistol under his pillow. Three weeks later they found his mother dead on the kitchen floor. The doctor called it a heart attack but Willy wouldn't hear of it. It was fear, he told his father and himself until both of them believed it was true. It was fear that killed her because until the night of the robbery she was healthy and strong and afterwards you could see the fear in her face. And one night last week, Willy told his father, he came home from work to find her awake, weeping alone in the chair in the corner of the kitchen. And it was near that chair, he said, that they found her dead.

Willy was ready for the next intruder, waiting with the loaded pistol under his pillow. He was almost asleep when he heard the first noise—a pile of canned goods being toppled—and for a minute he passed the noise off as part of a dream. But when he heard another noise he sat upright in his bed.

"Papa," he hissed. "They're here again."

He did not wait for his father to plead with him. With the pistol in his hand he charged down the stairs, only to face a black silence. Ducking behind a barrel of olives, he heard only the thick pulsings of his heart. He drew a deep breath and wanted to run but did not trust his legs. He waited for a sound, a movement. "But they're here," he said to himself. "I can smell them—like piss-stained old clothes." He crouched down further, trying to shrink. "I'll shoot," he finally shouted into the darkness. "I swear I will! I'll only run so far!"

The pistol in his hand was cold and wet. It felt small but as heavy as his arms and legs. He heard the stairs creak and he suddenly turned. "Willy, is he gone?" the old man said. "Willy, you OK?"

He didn't know why the sound of his father's voice made him leap out from behind the barrel of olives and run down one of the aisles toward the front of the store, just as he had nothing in sight as he began firing wild bursts until there was no sound in the store but the clicking of an empty chamber.

They heard no more noise in the store that night until the two police cars came screaming up to the front door. While neighbors gathered, Willy stood silent, holding the black pistol like a toy in his hand. "Can't figure it out," said the policeman. "No doors, locks, no windows broken. No money gone. And no damage except a few cans and boxes knocked over and bullet holes in the front window."

The policeman came back the next morning and looked around again. They said the bullet holes in the window came from Willy's gun, and they said they found a chunk of liver sausage that looked as if it had been chewed by a huge rat. They took it with them.

They drove by the next day and through the window of the patrol car gave Willy the good news. "That was no man in your store two nights ago. It was one helluva hungry cat you scared the hell out of with that gun of yours."

"You can't say that," Willy yelled at them. "How do you know? How do you know? How can you say that?"

"Ever see a burglar who shed cat hair?" the officer said as he handed Willy the liver sausage. And then they were gone without even listening to him.

Then the man who had been selling them protection for thirty dollars a month stopped in and told them to take out a mortgage or move within a month. The boss, he said, wanted to sell. That night Willy and his father talked. They had the four thousand dollars and another two in the bank, so late that night they decided to buy, both of them uneasy but glad. The next morning the man came with a lawyer who explained everything. And then they signed.

A week later Willy noticed bulldozers in the open lots near the corner of the block. "What's going on?" he asked one of his customers.

"They say it's going to be a supermarket," the customer replied, neither of them imagining yet what this meant. Nor did Willy understand when his father said simply, "We've been cheated."

A few days later he heard a screaming police car speed by the store. "What's going on," he asked a passerby.

"Don't know for sure," a boy on a bicycle said. "But it's probably them."

"Them?"

"Sure. Was some niggers moved in two blocks away last week. They say the neighborhood's going downhill. Pretty soon they'll be all over."

The boy was right, Willy thought as he saw them come and go from the supermarket. They'll eat that lunch meat and white bread, he thought, and they'll drive all the way here from the other side of Grand Boulevard to get it. They don't come in all at once. They sneak in one by one and then the neighborhood gets dirty and all the hard-working people go downhill.

He hated them, even the bent-over black lady who bought a package of bologna on the day they decided to call it quits, and especially the ones who crowded through the store the week before they closed their doors to get the special deals. At the end of that week Willy retreated from half-empty shelves to the back room. *They* did this, he thought to himself, and *they* were the ones who had broken into the store that night when he chased them out with the gun. And *they*, he vowed, would pay for it.

II

Six months after they closed the store Willy was looking for a fight. His father told him to get a better job and a wife. The factories were not hiring, so he lingered on in the kitchen where the only women he saw were the waitresses who blamed him for everything, and the black one, the boss's girl, who never spoke but smiled every time she rubbed past. His father collected Social Security and together they made ends meet.

When the army recruiter told him he could get his high school diploma and maybe become a cook, without telling his father Willy signed. He'll tell me not to, he thought, just like he told me not to buy a gun.

He took the gun everywhere, hiding it in the small pocket of a jacket he carried over his shoulder like an empty sack. He kept the gun hidden through basic training, and when he left for Vietnam he hid it in one of his bags.

The officers put him in the kitchen after he walked into the base trembling because of the night he spent in the jungle. They could see from his eyes that they should not ask too many questions. Even though two soldiers saw him run, they never said a word. Colonel Otterby said, "He looks like the type who belongs in a kitchen. Put him in the kitchen."

So Willy became proud of his soup. He stood defiantly by his big pot, hovering over it with a wooden soup spoon that looked like a club. For a whole year he never got a complaint—not until he had an argument with the big black soldier who spoiled almost everything.

But it was the cat who spoiled his sleep. Willy sat on the back steps of the messhall waiting for it, his pistol hidden beneath his apron. Still the cat was never more than the shadow of a presence mingling with the other shadows cast by the single lightbulb above the messhall steps. "He comes from out there," Willy told the cook, "from one of the villages in the hills."

He gave up trying to shoot the cat only after the rounds he fired recklessly into the trash barrels aroused the whole camp one night. Then he tried other ways. He tried poison first, even though it took three weeks to get it. "For rats," he told the men, and yes he had a secret plan for getting gooks to eat it too. But the cat wouldn't go for it. Willy mixed it with some chopped liver he cooked in a skillet, and he placed it on top of a heap in one of the barrels. But the cat turned up his nose at it.

Then he tried making a trap. He pieced bamboo sticks together to make a cage like the one the enemy had fixed over the head of Butch, a soldier someone had found dead hanging in a tree. Willy caught a mouse in the kitchen, and each morning for a week he awoke hoping to find the cat in the cage. At night Willy heard rummaging in the trash and each morning he found the mouse gone.

But he did not give up the idea of destroying the cat. The cat had passed into his night, lurked in his sleep. It was outside his own kitchen. And in the room when the men made him go to the whorehouse in Saigon. And the cat, his eyes on him, was on the prowl the night he spent nine hours lost in the bush praying for the sun to rise so he could find his way back home. "Someday," he vowed, "I'll get that goddamned cat."

III

One day the soup didn't taste just right. He tried adding salt. Maybe no one will notice, he thought as he wheeled the big pot from the kitchen. Or maybe it's me. Maybe my mouth is sour.

This made better sense to him. When the men came through the line, he watched their faces for a sign, and he did not ask for thanks. Nothing happened until the big black soldier from Chicago paused before the bowlful Willy handed him in silence, looked deeply into Willy's eyes and said, "There's a hair in my soup, Willy."

The surprise moved through Willy slowly, moving upward from his stomach to a burning point of focus in his brain. "Not in *my* soup," he said calmly, as if that ended it.

"Look again, Willy," the black soldier said.

"The name is William."

"But there's a hair in my soup, William."

"*Where*? Show me."

Jones dipped his fingers into the soup and, after probing a moment, lifted it out. Clinging to his wet forefinger was a black hair.

Willy leaned over the finger without touching it. The soldier moved his finger closer to Willy's face. "It's a hair alright," said Willy. "But it's your own hair. It's one of *your* hairs." That settled it. He reached for another bowl for the next soldier in line.

"Now William, you *know* that ain't one of my hairs. You know that's a cat hair or something."

A cat hair. The words sneaked up on Willy from out of the dark in the back of his mind.

"Soldier," he said, "I know that ain't cat hair. That's one of *your* hairs, soldier."

"William," said Jones, "you ever seen a cat with kinky hair?"

Willy searched his memory.

"When you find one, William, you show him to me, 'cause I ain't never seen a black dude got hair like this." He smeared the hair onto the table.

Willy wiped off the table and, as some of the men backed up in line gathered for a look, enclosed it carefully within the folds of a towel.

"William," said the soldier, "I make you a deal. You take this soup and give me more. Then I move right along."

"There ain't no hair in that soup, soldier, so you move right on!" He lifted the big wooden soupspoon off the table.

"William, we brothers. All I want is a bowl of good clean soup."

The words came before Willy could stop them. "You niggers are pushy—that's what you are."

Jones grinned, as if he had expected it to come to this. Willy took the bowl from him and set it aside. Then he took a clean one and spooned some soup into it. The soldier looked down into it. "Willy, it's only half full."

Willy's answer got lost in the crowd beginning to gather. While the two stood face-to-face over the half-filled bowl of soup, a hush fell over the front table in the dining hall and a few soldiers found their way to the other side of the serving table where they stood like a chorus behind Willy. Not until someone whispered the word "nigger" did the black soldier turn and face the crowd. "Come on," someone goaded him. "Come on, do something about it."

And then with one smooth motion the black soldier turned, scooped the half-filled bowl of soup within the palm of his hand, and slammed it upside down on the table. Just then an officer fought his way through the crowd.

"What's your name, soldier?"

The black soldier paused as defiance curled into his smile.

"Jones."

"Didn't they teach you to say, 'sir,' soldier?"

"Suppose they didn't."

"*Sir!*"

"Suh," Jones whispered.

"Your first name, soldier. What's your first name?"

"Lincoln. My name be Lincoln Jones." And he added another "suh."

"Do you realize you're causing trouble here?"

Jones stood in a lazy silence that said he heard all this before. The officer waited for a response, but Jones said nothing. "I want you men to disperse and resume your normal activities. I want no recurrence of this behavior. And you, Private Jones, are to have no role in further disruptive activities. You men clear a way here and let's all get in line and keep it moving."

The men opened a way for the officer. Jones moved down the line and did not look back when he heard Willy have the last word. "He'll be watching you," Willy said, "and so will I."

IV

Willy had been watching them for years. When he was a boy in New York he looked too long into their faces and eyes. One of them, his mother said, raped Mrs. Speranza, and another held a gun next to his father's ear the second time he was robbed.

Willy watched them after he moved to Detroit, especially when he rode the bus to work. The women, many old and weary, collapsed into the closest seat from the sheer weight they carried, a weight heavier than the bags that loaded them down. And the men, curled up into themselves with half-opened eyes, leaned their heads against the windows of the bus, indifferent to the jolting of the stops and starts. They all followed Willy with their eyes, and they all got off before he did and disappeared into the streets.

It didn't occur to him that they were coming closer, even when one of them rode with him to his stop, got off with him, nodded, and limped the opposite way. But when the supermarket moved in he watched them come in cars, and he watched them go away with bags bigger than any he had ever packed in his store.

He noticed one in particular, the girl who worked as a cocktail waitress at the restaurant and who just before closing left with the boss every night. He wondered about her until as she squeezed through the kitchen one night she rubbed herself against him. They should stay with their own kind, Willy thought, remembering only the crooked smile she gave him as she left with the boss that night. The smile made him turn away, but the warmth of her firm breasts against his body stayed with him until that night he fell asleep wondering what it would be like to move his hands over her face. She kept coming to the kitchen until he smiled at her one night, and for three nights his heart raced whenever he caught a glimpse of her.

It all ended before they spoke a word. One night she came as usual. This time she stared into his eyes, and he smelled her too—a sweet warm smell not of flowers or perfume but of flesh. She passed by him to the restroom and a few minutes later returned. Then Willy followed her scent until he found the half-flushed bowl and saw the blood-stained tissue. She kept coming back after that but he never looked up, even when in her last effort he heard her whisper his name as she squeezed by.

He also had been watching them since he had been in Vietnam. They always sat apart. When they were alone they sulked about, sullen in their silence. When they were together in their corner they made noise, and, more important to Willy, they made a mess.

"It's not our mess," one of them said to Willy after he told them to clean it up. "We don't own any part of this mess," he said while the others laughed.

To Willy it was a lie and he complained to the chief cook. "They're dirty and lazy," Willy said to the other men, and they agreed, hardening into silence when any of the blacks came near.

The men went out of their way for Willy. Only once did they make him do something he didn't want to do. It began when Willy learned that some of them had four-day passes to Saigon, and he asked to go along. They knew he would spoil their fun, but agreed they owed it to him.

Willy wanted to turn back as soon as he hit the streets of Saigon and saw the crowds. The cars and cycles buzzed between the people in the streets, and occasionally an American car bullied its way through. Twice during the day sirens screamed overhead but the traffic was unmoved, the faces in the crowd stolid, certain that the rockets were not for them, that rockets could leave pockmarks in the flesh of their city but that in time their human mass and movement would cover the wounds.

He spent the first afternoon wandering under a heavy heat along the sidewalks. Little men in coned hats leaped out at him to hawk their wares, while within the shadows of corners and doorways along the sidewalks old men sat cross-legged begging with their eyes. Children demanded favors from strangers, and girls with painted smiles stood in empty doorways. He turned away from a black-haired child in a gray garment squatting over her urine in a doorway. The traffic moved not in lines but in swirls, and the exhaust of engines seemed to stick to the yellow heat.

He wanted to go home—back to the kitchen and away from the confusion of these streets and people, back further to his mother and father and the grocery store. But he walked on with the others past the crowds and traffic until they came to a patchwork of shacks crowding each other in confusion, some of them built over a ditch. "Slums," Willy said to himself. "But much worse than Detroit." Before he could turn away with the others, he saw them: the little people, sullen, sitting knotted up into their skinny selves and sulking in a resignation filled not with hate or fear and least of all yearning, but only with the despair of waiting for the dignity that comes from expecting nothing.

The men turned back to the streets. They bought Willy a dinner in a small cafe, and they declined when he tried to buy the champagne. They said they owed it to him. Within an hour they finished three bottles of champagne. Then they began buying cocktails served by the women who asked them to dance. Everyone but Willy danced. Near midnight, when the three of them came back with a fourth woman, he knew they would make him do it, even before one of them leaned over to whisper that they already had paid for her.

They all went their own way outside the cafe. As the woman led Willy through the streets he did not see her lower her eyes as the Vietnamese men passed them, staring not at him but at her. She led him to a room at the top of a long flight of stairs: it was a narrow place six blocks from the cafe furnished only with a bed, table and small lamp. After she closed the door behind them, they faced each other in silence until her eyes opened into a smile. He looked at her deeply for the first time and saw her small face, narrow sleepy eyes and full lips. As she removed her robe, letting it drop down past her knees to the floor, he laid eyes on his first naked woman, her dark flesh yellowed by the dim light. And before she extended her arms toward him, he realized that he was trapped, that she stood between him and the door.

She said something before she moved toward him. While he stood helpless she began touching his neck and face, and he saw that her eyes were closed. There was nowhere to go, no way to escape the hands wandering over his body. He felt her moving downward to her knees, fumbling with his zipper with one hand and with the other taking his hand and touching it against her long black hair. Then suddenly he flamed into words: "Don't touch me, you dirty whore!"

She did not see his hand coming soon enough to ward the blow off, but in an instant her eyes narrowed and she leaped back away from him, her hands raised. When she saw his limp arms and vacant face, she drew herself to her feet and began screaming. He finally bolted, running down the stairs and past the faces appearing out of dark places.

Later the men asked him about it, even while he stood stonefaced, only his eyes showing the disgust he felt even for them because they had made him do this thing.

"Did you get some, Willy? Hey boy?"

"Did she put it in her mouth, Willy? I bet Willy *ate* her, eh men."

And they laughed, snickering even when he snapped on the small bed-lamp and turned away from them to face the wall.

V

They believed that Willy forgave them when they heard him speak from behind the pot of soup. For a month he had not looked them in the eye. They think I'm a coward, he thought each time he saw them. They think I'm a coward because I ran a second time, first in the jungle and then from the whore.

He remembered little about that night in the jungle. No one had slept the night before in the camp. He had lain awake cursing the lizards and their persistent "FOOK-OO" cries, and the next morning there was a heaviness in his eyes and an early morning sickness that sank him into an indifference deeper than his desire to live. If it had happened then, Willy thought, if they had walked right up to him then and shot him in the face or heart, he would not have winced. He would have welcomed this chance to abandon his life as a man welcomes his bed after a long pointless day. But like the lizards who ceased their crying as soon as the men began to stir, the enemy hid in silence waiting to strike in the heat of day.

As soon as they were all within the thicket of trees he saw the face of the man in front of him explode, and as he turned he saw the man behind drop even before he heard the fire. Then he dropped his rifle and ran until he fell to the ground face-first. He lay resigned, waiting for pain to rush through him and thinking with relief that this finally was the end, that there was a justice in it that made him equal to the men he had seen fall. He did not know how long he lay there or how many minutes or hours passed before silence fell over the forest. When he found the courage to raise his head, he saw bodies strewn on the jungle floor, some of them facing the sky and others face-down as if comfortably asleep.

He did not touch anyone. He walked past them slowly, his eyes fixed in a pointless stare that saw nothing but the spaces beyond the vague foliage ahead of him. The fear hit him later. "The wounded," he said out loud. "They'll come back to kill the wounded." He remembered the stories now—the tales of how they came back for the wounded or else waited for the rescue crews to come and then hit the crews. And then he was running, his legs heavy as stones carrying him nowhere except away.

He ran until his legs became tangled in weeds. Then he walked until the jungle was so thick he could not see the sky. He heard nothing, not even the lizards. He sank down behind a bush, slipped his gear off his shoulders and began fumbling for the pistol. He drew it out and it felt heavy and strong in his hand. Then he leaned back against his gear. Overhead the trees converged, and a slight breeze swayed them and let streaks of light break through. He would wait until he heard them come for him. They would send choppers out for him and when he heard them he would show himself.

But he heard no choppers all afternoon, and when the light began to fail in the evening and the lizards began their chorus again, the fear began to descend. Then as if a lightswitch had been thrown, he was lost in night, a black blank his eyes strained to see through. He looked up but saw no sky or stars. Even the tops of trees were lost. He heard sounds he had not heard during the day, a rustling between the silences that sent shivers through him.

He waited, straining to shake off the damp that made his whole body shudder. He kept the pistol in his hand, but his grip went limp. He did not feel the warm glow spreading in his pants until he smelled the odor of urine coming up through his opened shirt. As the urine turned cold, he tried to warm his body with his hands. He closed his eyes, and nothing changed.

Until he saw them. The eyes—wide, empty and slanted—leering at him from the darkness, staring down smugly at him from the branches of trees. They found me, he said to himself. They've been sitting up there all night.

He discovered the pistol in his hand, and began running his fingers along the smooth short barrel. The urine sent another shiver through him and before he could stop himself he began firing wildly until no sound came from the pistol but a dull clicking against an empty chamber.

When the flashes of fire from the pistol disappeared, he was alone in the dark. The jungle fell silent for a moment, but then responded with its own sounds. No, he thought, this can't be, and the thought became a single word "NO" that he began saying over and over until it was a howl filling the night with a terror that silenced even the lizards again.

Until dawn broke there was only silence and Willy cowering against his backpack as if it were a wall. When some soldiers found him the next day limping along the road just outside the base, he shivered and said nothing, and they saw the blankness in his eyes. So when they put him in the kitchen to make soup, no one complained. Willy had done his duty. And even though he slept with a small bedlamp shining on his face all night, he wasn't crazy. They agreed he wasn't really too different from the rest of them.

VI

They got to like him even more when he finally got his way. He had to run, and they knew it. The stories had come back with the survivors of that patrol. But the men knew that they too might have run and that to forgive running was a show of strength. The others should have resented him for being rewarded with a safe job in the kitchen, but except for a few they smiled at his ability to get what he wanted.

The victory over Lincoln Jones was easy enough. For when Willy stood behind his big potful of soup, he seemed to be in control of the stuff of life. Willy was often seen bending over his potful of soup whispering in an officer's ear, sometimes insistently. So it took only an excuse to trap Lincoln Jones. The men in the soup line could see Willy working his will if they were close enough to see Jones' eyes when Willy handed him his bowl each day. For the bowl was over half-full. Willy took pains to make everyone see that. And every day Jones leered at him through a smile, and, as he moved down the line, made a formal bow toward Willy as if to acknowledge Willy's gesture and add it to an account he was keeping. No one was surprised when it was learned that Jones had been sent to the stockade.

There was nothing left after that but to get the cat, which Willy did one night all alone. Almost everyone at the base knew something was up between Willy and the cat because every night for almost a week they heard the cat howl, each night the howl becoming louder and so mournful that the men who were awake wanted to cover their ears, and those asleep awoke to a fear that a baby was being butchered outside their windows. On the seventh night there was no howl. The next morning when they went to the messhall they found the charred carcass of the cat, skinny as a dried fish, tied head-down by its feet on the clothesline Willy used to hang his white apron on. After the meal a crowd gathered behind the messhall to hear Willy tell about it.

"After the right idea came," he said, "it was easy. You just have to out-smart 'em, so I did. So I said to myself: 'Well, I'd tried shooting it and couldn't hit it—just like it had nine lives. And I tried caging it and it wouldn't stay put, and I tried poison but it wouldn't eat the food.' So I says to myself, 'I'll starve it first and then burn it because burning's a sure thing.' That's what I said. I said I'd take it off welfare—that the thing's been living off the rest of us too long, that it's time to cut it off and make it work for a living. So I started scraping the cans clean. That's what I did. Then it hit me that I should wash 'em, and those last few nights there wasn't nothing in those cans to lick but a few drops of dishwater. But that was just the first part, 'cause I knew it would keep coming back only for so long. So I rigged up a trick. I got me a can of gasoline and I put that open can in the middle of all that trash. And then I just sit here on the porch smokin' a cigarette and waiting for the noises to begin, and I waited for it to thrash around in there a while and get in real deep before I just creeped up real close and flicked the cigarette in the trash. Then I just watched that old fire go 'Whoosh.' That's when I knew I had that mother-fucker. When I saw that trash-heap go up like a city, then I knew I had it."

"Hey William," one of them shouted. "You going after big game now? I hear there's still an old tiger or two out there in the bush that ain't been killed yet." And they all laughed.

"No siree," said Willy, "I didn't even wait for the fire to burn because I knew I had it. I just took me home, put out the light, and had me a good night's sleep."

ZABEL'S CHOICE

For over a year Zabel exchanged glances with the man across the bar from him, but he did not know if the man was enemy or friend. Zabel could only conclude one thing: the man had done enough drinking there to own the place.

The man was forty, maybe fifty-five. The lines on his face showed a sharper gray when he looked up. Like Zabel, he had his own place, the high stool near the back of the oval bar from which he could glance across at Zabel and see the door. He came and went every night, but Zabel, who left before midnight, did not know when. The bartenders, though new on the job every other week, kept the man's glass full without being asked. He wore old work shirts, a button missing here and there. And when he thought Zabel wasn't aware, he watched his every move. A friend, Zabel thought, maybe he wants a friend.

But they never exchanged a word. More than once Zabel caught him looking his way, then quickly turning away. Maybe there was nothing to his glances, Zabel thought, for all eyes in this particular bar appeared, took a few turns around the room, and disappeared. Still, Zabel was disturbed. The man's eyes maybe had a secret malice in them.

What Zabel hated most was the carpeting, a thin scarlet plush so foul from spilled drinks that his shoes stuck when he walked. He wanted to complain, but bartenders came and went overnight so he never knew who owned the place. Like the faces that sat around the bar every night, the bartenders were different but there was nothing new in them. Only the face of the man across from him, a face that neither smiled nor complained, remained the same. We have something in common, Zabel thought, or why would we be here every night?

Zabel came to the bar late in the night when few faces were left. He could give no good or bad reason for spending an hour over two beers. He was twenty-three years old and rented a room in a big old house three blocks away, but the carpet in that house did not stick to his shoes. He sometimes had a job but nothing he cared about. He was lonely but had nothing to say. Maybe he was looking for the perfect girl, but he would not find her in a place like this. And the dead smoke that purled under the dim overhead lights somehow soaked into his clothes, and he hated laundering his shirts just to get rid of the smell. He could have gone to one of the other three bars on the block, but he only could see himself, his feet propped on the cross-piece of the barstool so they would not stick to the carpeting, sitting in this place night after night. He knew he should visit his mother more often than he did, for she was all alone. But she worked so hard she seemed too tired to stay awake. She warned him about drinking too much, about giving his hard-earned money away for booze. It was that, she said, that brought his father to ruin. He threw his life away, she said. He just gave his life away to the men who fed him poison and gave him nothing in return for it.

Still Zabel returned night after night. At least the bar was oval-shaped. Even if his back was to the door, at least he could see everyone else from where he sat.

But one night he suddenly resolved never to return again. It happened when he took his usual seat and looked up to find no one sitting across from him. He looked around in confusion, saw other faces that came and went. Then, as if materializing out of the heavy smoke suspended in the room, appeared the strange well-known face of the man who had looked at him so many times from the other side of the bar. "Is there anything I can do for you?" the new bartender asked, opening into a smile that showed gold fillings in his teeth.

For a moment Zabel thought he had gone insane, had walked into the wrong room. He looked across the bar to the other place. Sitting there was a thin-faced boy in a dirty white shirt. He was no more than eighteen, his hair black and his eyes nervous with fear.

The new bartender leaned in close to Zabel, whispering. "Who's that creep sitting over there?"

Zabel shrugged, he did not know. Yes, yes, he wanted a beer, but before the bartender returned Zabel was gone. That night he pulled the blankets over his head, shivering and terrified. But he was not sure why he was afraid.

From that time on his life seemed relived. He had a toothache, a throbbing way back in his mouth from a tooth he could feel only with the tip of his tongue, and he dreaded the dentist's chair. It was there, in the dentist's chair, that he resolved to join the army after all. As he lay back in the chair waiting for the dentist to come into the room, he remembered telling his mother and sisters, everyone, that he hated going to the dentist, and now here he was in the dentist's chair, and the dentist had not yet even begun. During that two-minute wait he made up his mind to join the army, and he knew that nothing would ever change his mind again.

So he found himself circling the airstrips, the plane tilting now and then to give him a glimpse of the landscape below. The land was as he imagined it—but greener, the runways below thin ribbons of gray cut short by a dense foliage that flowed on and on further than the eye could see. The airplane circled for an hour before being given clearance to land, and every time Zabel closed his eyes he saw the same view.

So here I am, he thought as the plane taxied to a stop.

He was not afraid when out on patrol. Sergeant Schroeder warned everyone about the possible dangers. "Don't trust anyone or anything," he said. "There's boobytraps everywhere, and a nine year-old kid will lead you right to a land-mind that'll blow you to kingdom come."

I'll keep my eyes open, Zabel told himself before his squad moved through the bush. There were a hundred, a thousand, possible dangers. There were the trees, thick and full, a face lurking behind each broad leaf. There were tunnels everywhere, red eyes in them watching his every move. He had to watch his step. Beware a twig sticking in the ground. Or a sudden shot ringing out from behind, a shout, one glimpse, too late, of a boy escaping on foot. A whistling scream overhead, the shell landing before he had time to move. A woman, a brown-eyed girl, luring him toward the hootch.

"What would you do?" Schroeder asked over and over again. "Would you have the guts? Would you have the balls to blow her away before she takes you on a walk that blows you to kingdom come?"

Lund, a soldier who seldom said anything except with his knowing eyes, reassured him. "Schroeder just talks that way because he wants everyone to be real careful. He's just trying to take care of you. He's really on your side."

Schroeder, always careful and slow, led the way time after time. Let's just get it over with, Zabel told himself. Let's hurry and get it over with. What he hated most was walking through the muck. The muck would not give up its hold on him. It made him feel old and weak, and leeches got inside his boots. Back at the base he liked to feel the wooden wall of the barracks firm against his back. Even in the dead heat of night he pulled the blanket tight around himself.

This wood's nothing, he thought. They could shoot right through it like it was paper. Still he felt safer with his back against a wall.

Schroeder was everywhere. He nodded as the men stood in line for their food. He smiled when a private saluted him. On a Sunday morning he called Lund over and whispered something in his ear. One-by-one he cornered the members of his squad. "What would you do," he asked, "if you found a tunnel out there? If there was only two of you?"

Zabel found a tunnel one day. The rest of the squad was ten yards ahead. No, no, he argued with himself. It's not a tunnel, it's not. He looked at it again and froze. Maybe it was just a hole. There were red eyes in it looking out at him. He ran to catch up with the group, his heart pounding so wildly that Schroeder turned and glared at him. He knows, he knows, Zabel thought. Schroeder knows I passed the tunnel up.

"When you go into a village," Schroeder said, "you really have to be careful. There's gooks everywhere, and you don't just walk in and make yourself at home in a hootch."

"Then what do you do?" Kennedy asked.

"You do what you have to do," Schroeder said.

Schroeder never told anyone his age, but he had graying hair. He had a medium build, looked tired except when he shouted at his men. There were moments when he walked uncertainly, seemed to waver. Maybe he drinks too much, Zabel thought.

"Do you think we'll win the war?" Zabel asked Lund one night. "Do you think we'll ever be done with it?" Lund only shrugged. He didn't know.

Then one day the squad captured a VC. He would be skinny, Zabel thought, skinny and with uneven teeth. And his shirt would be hanging out, a plain shirt. His eyes would be afraid, but not full of fear.

The VC stuck his head out of a hootch and Kennedy saw him first. "Hey you!" he screamed as he fired rounds wildly at the hootch. The VC, a boy maybe fifteen, walked out with his hands in the air. His shirt had no buttons.

Kennedy, still ashamed, kicked him in the thigh.

"Who do you think you are?" Schroeder screamed as he grabbed the boy by the hair and bent his head down. "Who in the fuck do you think you are?"

The VC boy did not understand a word. Kennedy kicked him again, and Zabel saw the fakery in his wince, the pain on his face no cover for the hate hardened behind his eyes.

"Maybe the bombing will help our side," Lund said when Zabel asked again.

"What are you doing?" Zabel asked as he watched Kennedy take a grenade from his belt.

"I'll show you what," Kennedy said. He pulled the pin, held it a moment in front of the VC boy's eyes, and heaved it into the hootch. When it exploded the boy let out a cry as if he were the one inside, then he turned his head away and closed his eyes.

They ran away from the village with Schroeder leading the boy by a rope tied around his neck. So this is the way it is, Zabel thought. This is the way I thought it would be.

"What would you have done?" Schroeder asked everyone else the next day, and his eyes zeroed in on Zabel to accuse. "Would anybody here blame anybody else?"

"He's just trying to save our asses," Lund told Zabel again that same night. "He doesn't want to see any of his boys get hurt. He's just doing whatever he can. He's really on our side."

Zabel could not escape Schroeder's glare. Schroeder, arms folded, waited at the end of the food line. He walked through the barracks after the lights were turned off, pausing before every bunk. He took his place behind the chaplain at Sunday service. And when Zabel turned a corner, Schroeder appeared. In the messhall Zabel watched Schroeder eat. He looks like a pig, Zabel thought. His face is a snout. He gets his face too close to the gravy and meat.

One afternoon, just before three, Schroeder singled him out. "You, soldier," he shouted over the noise of a chopper descending on them. "Come over here and give us a hand."

The wind from the chopper blades sent a frozen chill through him. They want me to do something terrible, Zabel thought. I knew they would.

Before the blades stopped turning, the men in the chopper slid open the door. Zabel saw the cargo immediately. "Here, take one end," Schroeder said. Just inside the chopper door was a stretcher with a soldier on it, his face half-covered by a blanket. The chopper blades stopped before Zabel could make a move.

"He be dead," said the black ranger inside, his words too loud in the sudden silence of the afternoon sun.

Zabel knew what Schroeder had on his mind. That could be you, Schroeder's eyes said. That dead soldier could be you.

Zabel went to Sunday service again, he didn't know why. "Lead us not into temptation, and forgive us our sins," the chaplain concluded. The trees outside the perimeter of the base looked less green now, less dense. Zabel was a city boy, had never gone for a walk alone in the woods. His mother had been alone for years, still worked as a cashier in a supermarket. He remembered how the two of them took a drive in the country—"for a picnic," she said—just two weeks after his father died. He was only twelve then, and the picnic came to an end when he found his mother all alone, crying, under a tree.

Zabel imagined that Kennedy someday would get hit. Not because he deserves it, he thought. Oh no, not that. No one deserves to get hit. But Kennedy someday would get hit, because he had it coming to him. Kennedy laughed at the wrong time. Therefore he would get hit.

No more laughing, Zabel thought when he heard that Kennedy had been hit. "He was just standing there," said a soldier who saw it all, "and a sniper nails him from behind. Just like that. One shot. Right through the back."

Zabel imagined Kennedy's hanging face, his limp hands dancing over the sides of the stretcher as the men carried his body back. And he cried himself asleep.

Schroeder disappeared for hours. "He's taking it pretty hard," someone said.

There was only one thing for Zabel to conclude. Schroeder, he thought, will blame me, try to get even with me. He'll try to get even with me somehow.

Schroeder reappeared with a vengeance. "From now on," he shouted at the squad, "keep at least ten yards apart. And I don't want to hear anyone saying a word, not a peep. And when we get back from a mission I don't want to hear anyone talk about what happened. And you clean and check your weapon every night, even if you ain't fired a shot. And you shine your boots before you turn in."

"He's scared too," Lund said. "He doesn't want to get hit. He doesn't want any of you to get hit."

Then one morning, when Zabel was more than ten yards behind the soldier in front of him, he saw a leaf move in a tree to the side of the path. "Down!" he screamed, "Everybody down!" He himself was down, his fire tearing the tree to shreds before anyone heard his words.

When they gathered the courage to look, they found no sign of the enemy. "You goddamn idiot," Schroeder said. "You scared the hell out of everybody."

Two days later the squad emerged from the edge of a woods overlooking a rice paddy below. There were peasants working in the paddies, their stooped backs turned away from the advancing men. Then suddenly a cry went up and a woman in white, who had stood up to get a better view, started stumbling away through the knee-deep water.

"Get her! Get her!" Schroeder cried. "Get her before she gets away!"

The soldiers looked with confusion at each other, each waiting for the other to make a move. Schroeder looked back at his men, catching at last Zabel's eye. Then he lifted his weapon, took aim, and fired.

The woman suddenly stiffened, then fell forward face-first, disappearing into the muck. But then a hand appeared above the surface, thrashed in the water, and she pulled herself up.

Schroeder signaled for his men to get down, cover him as he advanced. The woman disappeared again, but in a few seconds she was thrashing above the surface again. "Keep down," Schroeder hissed to the men. Then he fired again and again.

Zabel and two others lifted her out of the water while the peasants watched. She was skinny, fifty-five years old. No, maybe seventy. She stuck to the muck, was almost too heavy to lift, and the water was brown with her blood.

"Let it be a lesson," Schroeder said. "You can't trust anyone here."

Therefore, it's just a matter of time, Zabel told himself again and again, before Schroeder nails me too. He saw himself laid out the way he imagined Kennedy. He saw the boxes piled against a wall in a warehouse, and he saw some of them loaded into transports for the journey home. Yes, he thought, maybe I'll be in one of them. Maybe I'm not so different from anyone else. Maybe it's just a matter of time. And maybe it will be better that way.

"I don't know what I'm going to do," he told Lund. "Schroeder's crazy and he won't leave me alone."

"Nonsense," Lund said as he threw his arm over Zabel's shoulder, "live and let live."

From then on Zabel tried to stay out of Schroeder's way. Zabel was afraid that one day he would just walk away from the squad and disappear into the woods. But he was afraid he would lose his way. He was sure he had seen someone in the tree. He would not have fired for no reason at all. Maybe he saved everyone's life. And Zabel wondered if Kennedy would still be dead when everyone returned to the States, if Kennedy would meet him at the airport, and together all three of them—his mother too—would go for a ride in the country.

Every day Zabel had to load all the gear on his back—ammunition, rations, grenades, all too much to bear in the thickened heat. And every day Schroeder was waiting to lead them into the bush.

Then one Tuesday Zabel sat too long on the stool, his gear on the floor next to him, the door to the stall closing everyone out. He sat with his head in his hands, far from the thought of Schroeder waiting for him. Did his mother have a birthday coming up? Careful not to come within ten yards of himself, he followed himself down a narrow jungle trail. He had to watch out for suspicious sticks, and he was sure there were faces in the trees. But maybe today was Sunday, so maybe he was safe.

"Zabel! Get the hell out of there!" Schroeder was outside, pounding on the door. "Do you think you *own* the goddamn shithouse?"

Zabel buttoned up, threw the gear over his back. Somebody had pissed on the floor. His boots felt sticky underneath. Nobody had cleaned up the mess.

Schroeder gave him an accusing stare as he squeezed by to get in. "Do you think you *own* this place?" he asked again.

Zabel stood at the door, confused. No, he did not own the place. He did not know who owned the place. But Schroeder told him to get out and he got out. So who owned the place? he asked himself. He did not know, but he had no choice but to get out.

He finally wriggled a grenade free from his belt, looking around to see if anyone would see. Sure he was alone, he pulled the pin and for a moment held the grenade before his own eyes. "There are some things," he said out loud, "you can't just ignore. Some things you gotta do something about."

Then, with a swift clean movement of both hands, he opened the door and rolled the grenade on the floor inside. He had to be careful to get far enough away, not be seen or heard. He didn't want anyone to guess what he might do next.

THE MAN WHO CURSED
AND THE GOOD LUTHERAN BOY

"Jeesus," said Lund when he first heard Clausen's stream of words. After a while he walked away with his hands over his ears.

Freddie, the good Lutheran boy who worked in the laundry, at first could not believe his ears, but after a while he wanted to hear every word. Without letting anyone see, he leaned in close whenever he got the chance.

Lund, the farmer's son from Minnesota, was the only one who caught Freddie listening. Though Lund was a Lutheran who never went to church, he knew that Freddie was from a small Iowa town. They had something in common, he thought, so he took it upon himself to make sure Freddie got to spend his time safe in the laundry. "He's the type that could get hurt real easy out there in the bush," Lund whispered to Major Hornsby.

Hornsby, after taking a long look at Freddie's slender waist and shiny blond hair, agreed that Freddie was just right for the laundry. "We need more like Clausen in the bush," he said. And Lund nodded as if it were the natural thing to do.

Still he caught Freddie leaning toward Clausen. "Don't you get tired of listening to that shit?" Lund asked him one day. "Seems like he comes your way whenever he wants to let loose."

"Because he knows I never swear," Freddie said. "Because he's trying to make me like him, that's why."

"Then why don't you just turn your back on him, walk away?"

Freddie straightened his collar. "Because he's just another test, and I don't think he can make me go wrong."

Clausen caught Freddie in the doorway of the laundry the very next day. Freddie was holding a stack of folded white towels, and he seemed to inspire Clausen to take a stand on the laundry steps.

Clausen always had a three-day growth, but he was careful about trimming the goatee and moustache that seemed too sharp for his puffed-up face. "What's a gook?" Clausen shouted so everyone could hear. "You wanna know what a goddamn motbereating gook is?"

Clausen always began with a question, then waited for a crowd to gather around. This time he knew he had an audience, because most of the men

116

were boys who had never been in the bush, and they knew that Clausen was a real veteran, the kind who couldn't say no to signing up for another year whenever his tour of duty was done. So if anybody knew what a gook was, Clausen was the one.

He waited for them to gather close. "A gook is a slope, a slant, a sneak. He slithers sideways out of his mother's slimy stinkhole and the plain light of day is so much for him he can't take the sight of it. That's why he has to squint the rest of his life. He's a cross-eyed pig with a double asshole, and the biggest one of them holes is underneath his nose. That's because he don't know what end is up anymore. There's so much shit in that hole he has to swallow hard all the time just to keep it all down, like he was trying to swallow his father's scummy cock but couldn't get it all down because it tasted like a cherry lollipop that got stuck in his mother's twat one Sunday in church when the reverend minister couldn't pull it out with his tongue without waking everybody up. And that's why gooks turn yellow like chickenshit VD come and sneak around the way they do. That's what this war is all about, people like that."

"Jeesus," Lund said, turning toward Freddie who was halfway behind the door. "Everybody around here talks like that. It makes me sick after a while."

"He does it because he knows," Freddie said, "what the Devil is like. If anybody knows, *he* should know."

"People like that," Clausen went on. "It's people like that make us all sick. Gooks. That's why the only good gook is a gook that's been knocked up by a bullet."

Major Hornsby, who heard Clausen from afar, said "Amen."

After Clausen finished, Freddie just shook his head. "What I don't understand is why he's always talking about sex."

Lund, who was interested in the way peasants farmed rice, had another complaint. "What bugs me is that maybe some of those privates are going to take what he says out on some old man working the fields."

"But you can't be sure of them, can you?" Freddie asked. "Ain't it hard to tell who the gooks are?"

Lund had to nod. "Everything's fucked up out there. There ain't no telling a gook from an ordinary man."

Then one day Clausen drank so much whiskey he decided he had had enough. He just sat down on the laundry steps and wouldn't budge. "Because they told him he had to go out there in the bush again today and he don't want to go," someone told Lund. "Some gook almost shot his ass off last time, so he's calling it quits for good."

Hornsby put him in the pen where Colonel Otterby used to keep the German Shepherds. "You act like a swine and I'll treat you like one," he said. "And when you want to act like a man I'll let you out."

Clausen howled for three days and nights, and everybody complained because they couldn't sleep. "Hornsby, I ain't no ass-licker like you, because you started in down low licking asses and you been licking them all the way up the line, and you think the asses up there taste good because they got steak sauce in them. And that makes you want to lick more asses, Hornsby."

At midnight of the third day Clausen let loose with everything he had. "Hornsby! Hornsby! Do you know what you are, Hornsby? Do you want everybody to know? You're a dink Hornsby, a dink! When a dink blows his nose, Hornsby, he shits a green turd that smells like the cock his mother sucked right after she took it out of some colonel's ass. And then she cooks that green turd, Hornsby, and puts it in a plastic sandwich bag for your lunch, and you love it Hornsby, because you got so much shit in your head nothing smells or tastes like shit to you no more. Dig it, Hornsby! We know you dig it. We all know you sit up there on your toilet bowl eating what's in them plastic bags. We all know it because we see you getting fat in the cheeks and neck. We see you licking up every last drop in them plastic bags. Because you're a dink, Hornsby, and that's what dinks do."

The boys in the barracks heard every word and cheered until Clausen suddenly stopped.

"I wonder what they did to him," Lund said.

"All he ever talks about is crap—sex and crap. That's all he's ever got on his mind." Freddie rolled over on his side away from Lund. "I just want to get some sleep."

"I wonder what they'll make him do . . . if he keeps refusing to cooperate."

"They should put him away," Freddie mumbled.

"Maybe he's crazy," Lund said.

Freddie said nothing. He had pulled the sheet over his head and was fast asleep.

The next morning Clausen was in the breakfast line with everyone else. His eyes looked sunken and dark, but they still did a wild dance whenever he lifted them to look about.

"How did he get out?" everyone asked.

"Maybe he made a deal with Hornsby. Must be he promised to hold his tongue."

Lund could see that Clausen's eyes followed Freddie everywhere.

"You," Clausen hissed when he finally caught Freddie alone inside the laundry. "What are *you* going to be when you grow up?"

Freddie didn't look up, pretended no one was there. He had two hundred white sheets to fold, and he had fifty all done.

Clausen whispered. "You going to be a pimp when you grow up? You going to take some good white fresh pink Iowa meat girl, some corn-fed sow who ain't ever tasted cock-juice, and you going to send her out to do good works? *You?*"

Freddie kept folding white sheets.

"You know what happens to that meat? There's niggers out there, and Jews and gooks and dinks and good clean Iowa boys, and they see that meat and they want it all alone by themselves, and they never want it to walk away. They want it *dead*, boy. *You*. You going to be a pimp when you grow up?"

"I'm going to Luther College when I get back."

"You gonna suck Lutheran cocks and cunts, or you only gonna go after the Catholic and Baptist ones?"

"I'm thinking of going into the ministry," Freddie said promptly.

Clausen moved in so close Freddie could smell his breath. "Then you gonna save my stinking soul, preacher boy?"

Freddie had nothing to say.

"Here boy, touch this stinking olive drab." Freddie jerked his hand away from Clausen's and looked for an escape. But Clausen blocked the door.

"I'm not a pig," Freddie said.

"Because you're not a gook," Clausen hissed. "So let me tell you what you are if you're not a swine like me. You're the grand champion jackoff of the Milky Way, and your come never turns yellow on your sock or toilet seat, and when you sit you never shit because you like to see how long you can hold it in, and when your ass fills up all the way to your ears you just pray and all them turds just find some nice soft spot inside your balls to hide and then they all dry up to olive size so you can keep packing it in. And then when it all hurts so bad you wake up screaming in the night because your legs are too heavy to run any more, then you're fucked, boy, fucked real good."

Clausen backed off, looked Freddie up and down. "That's all I got to say to you, boy. You mark my words real good."

Within a week Clausen was gone for good. Freddie and Lund both knew something was up when they saw the chopper's slow return, the way it brooded under its own weight as it hovered, then strained to drop its load gently down.

"Wonder who got it today," Lund mumbled to himself as he hurried over to get a look, his heart hoping it was someone he did not know by name.

"Clausen," the medic said. "It's Clausen for sure."

"He was just walking along," someone said, "and he got nailed from behind. And then he turns around to see what happened and he gets nailed again. Then I don't know what happened after that. The rest of us, we just hit the ground."

Lund lost control of himself. "So them shit-eating motherfucking gooks had you on both sides?"

"We were surrounded by them."

119

They needed help unloading Clausen so the medic motioned to Lund. He had to help with the feet, had to carry him to the body bag already prepared on the ground. He couldn't believe how heavy Clausen was, and he couldn't get one leg to bend so they could zip up the bag. Someone else had to twist the leg into the bag because Lund's hands suddenly went limp.

A few waited for the truck to carry Clausen away.

"Poor fucking devil," Lund said over and over again. And he wept right in front of everyone.

Freddie had nothing to say. When he saw Lund weeping he turned away. "What's eating him?" he asked himself. Then he took one last look at the bag and slipped away to the laundry. "I got five hundred pillow cases to fold," he explained.

THE SNIPER

I didn't laugh when they told me. A sniper. I didn't laugh until I was up in a tree looking for gooks. And I didn't believe it then. I was from Chicago. Snipers were Japs. I was no Jap.

But the C.O. gave me the final word. "Things ain't how they used to be," he said with eyes that kept saying he was sorry, it was all too bad. "You gotta fight different now. This is a dirty little war. A stinking dirty war."

I still didn't believe it until I was up there in that tree about a mile from the base, and then I just cracked up laughing so hard every gook in China must have figured out where my hiding place was.

I never laughed loud or climbed that tree again. And there was no way to get out of the deal. "Because you volunteered for special duty," the C.O. told me when I complained, "and now you can't get out of it. You used your own free will."

He was right. So I guess I started thinking about whether I ever wanted to use my own free will again.

I felt ashamed the very first day. Like an ape—a grunt who has no business near a branch with birds. It was like being around pretty girls, or in English class, because I couldn't write too good.

So here I was up in a tree every day. I had to force myself to get out of bed for that, because once I was up in a tree I was all mixed up, worse than I was in bed. Sometimes, when the sun was out and the breeze was stirring just right, I would think there was nothing wrong in the whole wide world. I could see for a mile and a half and nobody could see me. I could watch a mama-san walking down the road with two little ones hanging on, and I could see the base with all the men looking small and slow, and all the trees were green, just washing back and forth like big waves. I would think everything is so peaceful I'm just wasting my time.

But then I would suddenly wise up. I could lose my grip and fall, and there were gooks down there sneaking around like snakes in the grass. If I didn't stay awake, keep my eyes open everywhere, I'd be dead as a duck. And the more I thought about these things, the more they scared the shit out of me.

121

Still, I tried to keep my cool. My second week out I found a little island of trees right in the middle of the boondocks. There were four trees bigger than the other ones here, and from the top branches the rest of the bush spread out beneath me like a lawn and I could almost look into the window of Colonel Otterby's office on the base. Three of the trees stood around the one I never climbed. This tree had a wrinkled hide like an elephant's and black branches that spread out so wide they seemed to hold up the sky. The tree reminded me of some old rocks I'd seen with fossils in them. I couldn't help thinking this tree was as old as the one in the Garden of Eden.

I kept coming back to these trees, then I started giving all but the grandfather tree names. Girl names. And I changed the names like I was turning pages in a magazine. Pepita. Gloria. Roxy. Carolee. Tammy. Baby Jo. Lori. Lynn. Sal. Every day when I got to the trees, I'd have a helluva time trying to choose. But sooner or later I picked one out and found myself a nice spot between big limbs and waited for the wind to kick up a little breeze. Then I'd just sway back and forth until I wised up to where I really was.

I think now I must have been crazy because I kept coming back to the same spot and didn't really see what was going on in the bush. At first I did. First two or three weeks, in fact. But I never saw nobody, and so I got to half-dozing off, just sitting there swaying in the breeze and watching the sky and wishing I could have a good smoke.

I wanted to tell the girl from Minnesota all about it but I knew she wouldn't understand. And because I knew she wouldn't understand I didn't want to write, even though I knew I had to. I put my name on that damned list and they sent the list to the States before I could take it off. I forgot about the list until about three months later. That's when I got a letter with her picture in it. The letter was too short. She told me she was nineteen, she was a college student at a college named St. Olaf, she had a father who was a doctor, and she had an uncle in the army, stationed, she thought, in Saigon. Then she told me all about the small town she grew up in, and finished by saying the war was a terrible thing—all wars are hell. She said she was writing because she didn't want our boys to feel lonely or homesick, and she wanted me to tell her about how I felt, only if I wanted to. And maybe, she said, we could become friends and get together after the war was over.

"Yours truly," she signed it, "Sandee Christianson."

Mine truly. I had to laugh at that every time I looked at her picture. I'd never seen anyone so pretty. She had blond hair and a perfect face, and every time she looked at me I felt like I was falling into the sky. I couldn't imagine her ever being sad. Now and then when I was up in a tree thinking about her, a little bit of hope would pass through me like a heartbeat. I thought, well maybe she's true. Maybe she wants to see me some day. Maybe.

I had to write her back anyway. I'd seen the C.O. go around with the list of names and he was asking all the soldiers if they wrote back. He kept saying you couldn't sign up for letters and then not write, and I figured he'd get around to me pretty soon. So I had to write, even though I'd put it off for over two weeks and never could get anything better than a "C" in my high school English class.

One night after I had been rained on all day out in the bush, I came back to my bunk and started writing. I reread her letter but I didn't take her picture out. I just wanted to get it over with, so I started writing anything that came to me:

Dear Sandee:

Well I guess this is going to be a trip. So dig it. The C.O. gave me this letter of yours and said write. Its cool. I'm from Chi-town and been in Nam now almost 10 months. Can't wait to get the hell out of here. I'm a Sniper for the 2/12 Cav. Don't really know how I got to be a Sniper. But here I am. Thought maybe you'd be from Ill. or Chicago. So if you wanted to we could party a little when I get home in July. I'm going on R. & R. next month to New Zealand. They say its like a paradise there. Can't wait. My R. & R. is from 15-22 Feb. After five months in this R. & R. is going to be a trip. Out of the bush then where I can get to see some real people. Dig it.

Yes, I could dig seeing some real people instead of sitting in some tree halfway asleep waiting for something to happen but hoping for nothing. Afraid to doze off because of the gooks. They probably could smell me right through the trees. Like the Japs. So you had to be careful. You'd be a fool to go back to the same tree. Like me. You had to fight their way. Their dirty stinking war.

When I came back from one of those trees I was always more afraid. After mess I'd lie down in my bunk, put on the earphones, and turn the music up so loud my ears hummed when I took them off to sleep. Sometimes I didn't sleep. I just lay there all night in the damp sheets listening to the lizards. I sometimes thought of the Minnesota girl. Even if I could find the words, I didn't want to tell her I was afraid. Because she wanted to hear about how I did my duty. Though there was no duty really—nothing like eating, sleeping, or even screwing, and nothing I had to do because I believed in it.

I only did what I had to do—such as climbing down the trees to piss, once in a while thinking it would be just my luck to be picked off in midstream. Once I did it in my pants because I thought there were gooks all around waiting for me just to come down. And one time my heart stopped because I heard something crawling around in the bush. I waited and waited, trying not to breathe, but I couldn't see a thing. I thought maybe it was behind me so when I turned I saw it, some sort of strange looking brown animal like a big rat taking turns on the small trees, chewing on the bark. I couldn't stop my heart from pounding for an hour after that.

But I was scared shitless when I saw a gook. It was weird because he wasn't very smart. He hunched down behind a bush maybe thirty yards away—I could almost see his face, and I knew he was scared. He kept looking around—behind himself all the time as if somebody was going to get him from there—but he kept inching right toward me. I knew there was no one behind him. When I saw him I wanted to tell him it was alright to turn around and go back, because there was no one there. But then I saw his weapon and I got so shook I just about slipped out of the tree. By the time I had my own weapon up and tried to get him in my scope, I was shaking so hard I thought he had three heads. I fired anyway, and he stood straight up right in front of me. I thought he saw me, but then I saw he was confused. He started looking around like he was lost, like he wanted to ask me which way to go, and then he just caved in, collapsed like a burlap sack you drop on the ground. By the time I put my weapon up to fire again, he was gone. Some brush parted like grass does when a snake goes through it, and that's the last I saw of him.

I've thought a lot about what became of him, and what it was he had in mind to ask me right after I shot at him.

Right after I was sure he was gone I started shaking again and had to get down out of my tree. I couldn't believe I really did something like that. It all happend so fast I started wondering if I *really* saw anyone. I couldn't believe how he just disappeared. Then I remembered those old movies again and I thought maybe this gook wasn't so dumb—maybe he was just acting to draw me out. Anyway, I was never the same after that. Some kind of secret spring broke in my mind when I tried to get the gook in my scope, and when I heard my fire rip the morning apart I felt like I cut the heart out of my little island of trees.

II

That's the way I felt when I thought about Evelyn, the only girl I ever had, and how she did me dirty. Trying to find a girl after Evelyn was no use. I never could put my heart in it. The girls always danced away full of smiles and left with somebody else. Sometimes I'd see them on the streets and want to stop and tell them I knew them from the dance. It was like trying to stop traffic. Sometimes I wanted to walk right up to them and tell them what I wanted, but mostly I was mad because they couldn't see it for themselves. So when they walked by without looking at me I just said fucking bitches to myself and watched them wiggle away. Then I started all over with my eyes, but none of the pretty ones would give me the time of day.

The girl from Minnesota was the prettiest one of all. Sometimes when I was sitting in a tree I'd take her picture out and look at it, and one time I caught myself talking to it. She was better than everybody else, but there were times when I was sure she was the worst. I'd look at her eyes and face and think of baby powder. I swore to myself she was just like the other ones, and I'd never be able to touch her. So when she wrote and I looked at her picture and said "just maybe," I should have known for sure. Even when I tried finishing my letter, I was fooling myself, because I knew the truth.

You sound real groovy in your letter. Sure would like to meet you but Minnesota is a little trip from Chi-town. On my 30 day leave in April I'll probably just party around home but if you could dig it and come to Chi-town. Well that would be cool. As you ask how the Army treats us. Well the food isn't fit for a dog and they work us just like a dog. I don't believe in this war one bit. But what can I say. I was drafted for two years. Either come in the army or go to jail for 5 years. So dig it. I played it out and pray to god I make it. I just don't dig killing people. I'm 22 or should say 23. My birthdays May 8. You said your uncle was over here Well he can tell you what its like. I'm half Italian and Irish. I'm 5'11" and weigh 170. Black hair, brown eyes. All the girls used to like me. That should give you a little appearance.

I thought a long time about saying anything more, and I could think of only one more thing to say but wasn't sure I should say it. So I folded that part of the letter and put it in my pocket. For the next two days I took it with me in the bush, and sometimes, when the breeze was blowing and I was just swaying in a tree, I had the urge to come down, sit back against the trunk, take her picture out, and tell her everything. But I didn't.

At the end of the second day I told myself I had to get rid of the letter. I felt it hanging on me all the time. I decided, what the hell, I'd add a few lines.

I had a girlfriend named Evelyn before they sent me here. She's a Puerto Rico girl, black haired, very pretty. We went together a year. Then I went back last X-mas to surprise her and she sure surprised me. I found her shacked up with another guy, a nigger from the southside. I'm not prejudice but I didn't dig it. She cried and said she was sorry and she wanted me back. But I said no dice, I wanted to find me a nice girl.

125

Well I'm going to sign off for now and try for some sleep. I hope you trip on reading this as much as I enjoyed writing it. If you'd like to tell me more about yourself it would be a trip. Give everyone there the peace sign for me and tell them its from Nam. Tell all the girls to stay sweet and all the GIs over here really dig them. I don't care what anyone says. American girls are the greatest and I've been around a little.

Well that's all for now.

Yours truely,

I signed my name, put the letter in an envelope and even put a stamp on it. But I still somehow couldn't bring myself to putting it in the maildrop. I put it in my pocket again and carried it out into the bush the next morning and every morning for two whole weeks before I finally decided what to do with it.

III

Then I got a visit from Willy Marcanti, the private who ran the messhall because he told everybody what to do in there and got away with it. He slid up to my bunk late one night and never raised his voice.

"I've got a deal for you," he said.

"A deal?" I said. I heard about some of his deals. He was in charge of food and making the soup, and we ate better than the U.S. Senate. We had clams and lobster and all kinds of Italian food because he was Italian. One time we had legs of lamb—everyone had his own leg—that came in big boxes marked "soupbones." Nobody could afford to eat the way we did, and that's why we thought he had a line to somebody big somewhere.

"A terrific deal," he said. "You're half-Italian, aren't you? I'm only letting a few in on it."

"A deal for what?" I asked.

"Souvenirs."

"Souvenirs?"

"Souvenirs of the war," he said.

"What kind of souvenirs?"

"Guns."

"Guns?"

"Sure. I got a whole truckful coming in—big ones, little ones, any kind you want."

"But what for?"

"To take home. Something to remember your tour of duty by. Something to give to your friends. Or you can sell them. They'll bring anywhere from fifty dollars to five hundred each. I promise you that."

"What are you selling them for?"

"Either three dollars or ten. They come in two classes only. The small ones are three, the big ones ten. And some of the big ones are real bargains."

"Where did you get them?"

"I don't have them yet. I'm just taking orders now. You get them thirty days after you order."

"How do I get them back to the States?"

"That's your problem, but it's easy. I can make a deal to get them back if that's what you want."

"I don't want any guns. What am I going to do with a gun?"

"Where you from?" he asked.

"Chi-town."

"That's what I thought. You got family there?"

"Yes."

"You sell your guns there. Listen man, don't be a fool. I'm from Detroit. The streets there are like a jungle full of cats, man. You got gooks there too, man." His left eye curled down. "You know what I mean?"

I knew what he meant.

"Don't be a fool. You buy five guns at ten dollars each and you got two thousand dollars in the bank. I'll have more next month and a way to get them back. You figure it out. Say you make deals for six months. You figure it out."

"I don't know," I said. "Where did you get guns?"

"I made a trade. See, they're not really anybody's guns. I made a trade with the people who sell food. The food belongs to us and the guns were part of a deal—a bonus. So the guns belong to all of us. I'm just handling them for us. All I want to do is break even."

"What's in it for you?"

"Do you men eat good here? That's what it is to me. We got a war on here, and I want to treat the men right. I hate them gooks as bad as you, and some of my men are going to get killed—maybe today, maybe tomorrow. I want every meal to be like a last supper."

I didn't believe it but I think he did.

"All you got to do is put your name on the list. You won't have to pay until Thursday."

I hesitated, looked away.

"Look here now," he hissed, "I just don't want to take a loss. I'm not doing this for just myself."

"Okay, then, okay. Put my name down, but just for one. I only want a small one."

"You're cheap for an Italian," he said as he scrawled my name on a yellow sheet. "But you know what you'll need in that jungle when you get back. I know Chicago's no better than Detroit, and I'll make sure you get one that don't miss even if you're shooting at nothing but the whites of their eyes in the dark."

"Sure," I said, "sure."

"Pay me now or in the messhall. No later than noon on Thursday. I'll be around back."

"I'll pay you later," I said.

As he turned to leave I noticed he hadn't shaved in a day or two and his shirt hung out behind. He looked tired and even dirty for someone who spent all his time in the messhall. And I felt dirty. I hadn't showered for three days. I felt the way people sometimes do when they take more food than they can eat and then just have to throw the leftovers away.

And I felt that way when I caught Evelyn shacking up with that nigger just before I joined up. "You filthy pig," I yelled at her, and I yelled it over and over, not even paying any attention to the nigger, big-eyed and scared, knocking over a chair to get out of the room. I felt dirty and rotten even though I kept hissing it between my teeth all the time Evelyn tried to explain to me and swore she was sorry and wanted me back. I felt dirty and rotten up to the moment I slapped her and told her to shut up because I had had enough of her filthy lies. Then after I slapped her she stopped crying and we just looked at each other a minute until I turned around and walked out on her without saying another word or even closing the door. I don't know what I felt after that. I don't think I felt nothing.

She sent me a letter after that begging me to come to Chicago on my R. & R. I only sent her back two words: "No deal." But I didn't feel good about it. I liked her too much, and she was the only girl I met who came right out with what she wanted. I wanted her back—I knew that. But I didn't know how to get her back without feeling bad about it. All I could think about was my R. & R. in New Zealand, my swimming all day and then drying off on the sand. After Willy left I daydreamed about it for over an hour, and I would have fallen asleep if I hadn't been hit by an idea. I jumped off my bunk, got out pen and paper, and began writing almost before I was awake.

Dear Evelyn:

I've been thinking about us. You want me to come home but I won't come home on R. & R. in Feb. If you really want me back you meet me in New Zealand on my R. & R. They say its a paradise there—ocean and beaches etc. We'll get a little apartment with a little stove and you can bake me one of those apple pies you always said you would make for me. Then we can see if it will work with us. I'm ready to forgive and forget.

Yours truely,

I kept it short because I wanted to sound serious, and then I slipped it in an envelope. But for some reason I couldn't walk over and put it in the maildrop. I remember I put my head in my hands and almost started crying because I could see her there in the sack with that nigger. So I didn't know what to do. I reached in my pocket and found the other letter, the one I'd had there for almost two weeks. The face of the girl from Minnesota flashed before me. Yours truly. I'd been thinking about Evelyn so long I'd almost forgotten about it. Now I had two letters to mail and I didn't know what to do. I put the letter to Evelyn in my pocket with the other one. I'll have to think about it, I told myself. Maybe I'll send the one to Minnesota but not the one to Evelyn, or the other way around. Or maybe I'll send both of them. Then I turned off the light.

IV

I slept on my options that night, not bothering to take off the jacket with the letters in it. But I didn't sleep long. The sound of a dog barking far off in the hills woke me up just as the sun was rising, and I spent about two hours there waiting for him to finish. Finally, I thought I heard some yelling way off somewhere and then the dog stopped barking. I wavered between sleeping for another hour and getting up, and the time passed until I heard some stirring in the barracks. Then I sat right up in my bunk, my heart crazy and my arms and legs scared stiff.

Right then I thought I must have been having a nightmare, but I wasn't sure. The noise sounded faint, about a mile away. If it wasn't a dream, then who was it? I got to thinking about myself all alone in a tree out in the bush—how I sometimes almost fell asleep because it was so quiet and serene, and how I used to ride my ladies one at a time when the breeze kicked up. This morning I couldn't think of passing the time that way, for I wasn't so sure I was alone out there.

I shaved like I always did and I checked my weapon and gear. I was drowsy and down as I made my way through the high weeds at the perimeter of the base toward the trees. I wasn't thinking very much and I didn't really care what would happen to me. I headed straight for my little island in the woods, for my ladies and the old man. Then I just climbed one of the trees—I didn't care which one—got myself comfortable, and sat back to watch the day go by. I could see it was going to be a gray day and I was feeling gray, so I decided I wasn't going to let a nightmare get to me because I didn't care about anything, not even getting home alive. This mood gets to all of us now and then, but it had been getting to me more and more. I decided not to fight it off. Fuck it, I said to myself. It's just the way I am.

I wasn't really too pissed off, but I wanted to hit someone and didn't know who. I thought of Evelyn and the blond from Minnesota, and I thought of Willy and his guns, and Otterby, who ran everything at the base and whose uniform never had a wrinkle on it. And I thought of a truckload of dead GIs brought back from an ambush and unloaded like they were crates of soupbones like the ones Willy fed us and called legs of lamb. I was tired of everything and couldn't even think of going back home or swimming in the sea off New Zealand on my R. & R. The only real thought I had was that maybe it would be nice if someone spotted me, picked me off, and got it all over with.

These were the thoughts I wanted the trees to hear—it was pillow talk of sorts. Now and then I'd wrap my arms around one of the branches and just hug it, and when the breeze kicked up a bit I felt her sway with me and heard the leaves whisper. I felt better when this happened, and for a minute I thought I'd stay out here for good and just never go back to the base.

My little dream ended when the breeze kicked up hard enough to stir the big old tree standing about fifteen yards from me. He creaked the way you hear old men creak sometimes when they walk around in old wooden houses. I couldn't help but look. And what I saw made my heart stand still. There, right under the old man's big lower branch, was a gook. He was one of the enemy, there was no doubt about that. He had those black pajamas and one of those pointed hats that left his face in shadow, and he was carrying a weapon and a belt of ammo slung over his shoulder. I hardly had to move my weapon to get him perfectly in my scope. I only had to squeeze the trigger without even looking, and he would be dead. That's how close we were.

I got my hands on my weapon alright, and everything happened too fast for me to get nervous. But I didn't fire. I didn't pull the trigger because he did a strange thing. He looked back over his shoulder away from me, then turned back toward me, stared me in the eye, and put his weapon on the grass. I expected him to raise his arms and surrender but instead he took his hat off and put it down next to his rifle. When I got a good look at his face—a skinny face about twenty or thirty years old—I realized he hadn't seen me yet. The breeze kicked up again and I was afraid the sound of the wind through the leaves would give me away. I would have shot him if he had not turned his back to me to see if he was being followed. I realized then he was afraid.

After looking all around one more time to see if he was alone, he untied a rope sash, climbed out of his pajamas, and laid them on the ground a few feet from where he stood. Naked, he was skinny and all angles, and small, like a boy. I half-expected him to climb up into the old tree and hang from a branch. He stood there another moment, his eyes sweeping by me, and looked confused, ashamed. He looked back over his shoulder a final time to see if he was being spied on. Then, like a Buddhist monk I had seen in the streets of Saigon, he squatted down. I saw his face strain, and a second later he took a crap.

I never saw anything like that before, though I suppose it isn't really strange. I only know I somehow had to keep from laughing. I relaxed my hold on my weapon a bit because I had to see the whole thing through. And he gave me no trouble. When he was finished, he got up, looked behind him again, took a few steps to one of the lower branches of the tree and picked off a few big leaves. Then he squatted down again and wiped himself. I'd never seen anything like it before. It was like catching someone making love.

But the show wasn't over yet. He wiped on two or three leaves and threw them up next to the old tree's trunk, but on his last wipe he seemed to smear some on his hand. He didn't seem sure himself, but he looked at his hand in a funny way. Then, glancing another look over his shoulder, he raised his finger up to his nose and smelled it. He held it there a second or two, moved it away to look at it, and then wiped it on the grass next to him. All the time he looked a little confused. Dig it, I said to myself.

Something clicked in my mind right then. Suddenly I knew exactly what I was going to do. I knew what I was going to do with that gook down there beginning to put his pajamas back on. I knew what I was going to do with the letters I had been carrying around in my pocket. And I knew what I was going to do from now on every time I had to come out here in the bush alone.

I let the gook get dressed. I let him sling the ammo belt over his shoulder and let him pick up his weapon. Then I let him walk right past me into the bush and out of my life. I remember thinking he might come back, someday it might be him up in a tree looking down at me, or if it wasn't me it might be somebody else like me. But I decided I couldn't help that. There were some things I couldn't be responsible for. There were some things you had to blame on God or the system. All I know is it wouldn't have been human to kill a man who had done that right in front of my nose. From now on I'd have to take my chances. The whole goddamned United States of America would have to take some chances.

Deciding what to do about the letters was easy after that. I took both of them out of my pocket and held them to a streak of sunlight coming through the leaves. I thought about the girl from Minnesota—how pretty she was, how happy she was going to her Bible college somewhere in the woods in Minnesota, and how she would never in a million years give me the time of day if she ever met me in the streets of a city. It's for girls like her, I thought, that we're fighting this war. It's so they can have peace and everything they want. And she wrote to me because she thinks it's the American way.

When I was sure the gook was gone I got down out of my tree and walked over to the place underneath the old tree where the gook had nearly laid down his life. The old tree looked wrinkled and gray, but there wasn't a bend in his big trunk anywhere. The ground under him was as soft as a bed from the drifts of leaves that had fallen and rotted there. I smelled the

131

gook's crap—a strong stink I couldn't stand. I bet it will help those leaves rot faster, I said to myself.

Then I took one of the envelopes out of my pocket again, tore it in half, and threw it on the spot where the gook had dumped his load. He could have used the paper a while ago.

Then I just started walking back to the base. It was still early in the afternoon, but I didn't feel like working any more so I thought I'd just meander on back. I'd take my time and take in some of the sights along the way. And I'd be careful too. I wasn't dumb enough not to be scared. In fact I had pissed in my pants again while the gook was squatting in front of me and I didn't notice it until I got down out of the tree. It was beginning to get cold, but it didn't smell bad. So I could still make a good afternoon of it.

And I decided that's what I'd try to do the rest of my tour. I'd come on back to my girls and old man every day and look after them. I liked it there and they agreed with me. I'd keep an eye open and not doze off. And I'd try to stay alive. There was no sense looking for trouble that didn't come my way, not in this dirty little war.

THE LIGHT AT THE END OF THE TUNNEL

There wasn't much I really could do all by myself. I could see the signs of the tragedy one at a time, but they didn't show themselves all at once. And when like a swift sword it struck, I wasn't even there. So there wasn't much I could do to save Sam.

I'll never forget the day he got the letter from home. "Well, I'll be," he said, "my kid sister had a baby girl." He looked confused by the fact it was a girl; he had never expected that. But for a week he flashed a picture of that baby girl to every soldier on the base, and though she was so small her eyes were still half-closed, everyone said she was a beautiful thing.

Except for that he wasn't much inclined to talk, and if he talked to anyone, I was the one. He was big, maybe six-foot-three, muscular from the neck down, though when he walked he was awkward and slow. He was somewhere between a man and a good big boy, and his eyes were as blue as a clear summer sky. He ate too fast and too much, seemed able to take everything in. Once, as he stretched after taking his fill, I could see that he had grown out of control, that behind his fine strong looks there was an untamed wilderness.

He had one habit that really pissed me off. He always had a coke or beer in his hand, could drink a half-dozen at a time. Whenever he felt like it he just took a piss—on a tree, in the middle of a road, on the tire of some jeep parked behind the messhall, even out a window if he could get away with it.

"Who in the hell's going to clean your messes up?" I complained.

He looked down at me with innocent eyes. "Aw, I ain't gonna leave but a yellow stain here and there. There ain't nobody's gonna mind too much over here."

Nobody minded too much. The best he could do whenever he felt the urge was to look around for me as if I was some sort of conscience following him.

He was easy enough to please. His idea of fun was to sit around drinking beer with the other boys, listening and laughing but never saying much himself. The loud ones liked him for that. When their show ended

133

they would dump him in bed. Then Sam would mumble things, sometimes throw up, sometimes pray and curse before falling asleep. That's mainly when I got to know his beliefs: he had none in particular and all of them at once. That maybe is why everybody liked him so.

Everybody also liked his hat. It was a cowboy hat of sorts, with a feather stuck in the band. He wore the hat every time he got the chance.

"That's a mighty fine hat," a lanky soldier said one night. "You from Texas too?"

"Naw," he said. "Ain't ever been there. Ain't ever been to Minnesota, where Lund's from." He pointed at me. "But someday I wanna go visit his farm."

His family had run its course from sea to shining sea, so he didn't know where he was from. "My mom and dad were from out east," but he didn't remember where, "then they moved to Ohio for a year and then Chicago, I think. And from Chicago we moved to some Kansas town, then Colorado and Las Vegas, and, ten years ago, I think, Long Beach. My folks are gonna retire someday," he told me. "They want to go to Tucson or Florida." So where he came from didn't matter the way it sometimes does. But maybe it mattered even more because it was as if he had touched us all somewhere along the way.

He got to Vietnam the way everybody else in our unit did: he was drafted six months after Vietnamization of the war began. Some of us were foolish enough to believe that Vietnamization meant we therefore wouldn't have to go. Even when I was on the plane, swept along on some jet stream thirty thousand feet in the air, I didn't believe I was on my way. Only when I was on the ground with everyone else did I really believe. But Sam believed right away. He didn't like it but he found being drafted easy enough to accept, and for him the fact that it happened was reason enough to be where he was. "Jesus Christ," he said, "they got a right to their opinion too." He was capable of that kind of faith.

I wish I had him back to talk about the way he died. I wonder if he'd say the reasons are simple and clear, or if he'd agree with me that only a few would understand and not many be willing to believe.

I once asked him if he was afraid. "I mean when you were drafted. Were you afraid you might be killed or something terrible would happen to you?"

He looked at me as if I was wrong to ask a question like that. "Naw," he said, "I wasn't scared. But it was weird."

"What was weird?"

His eyes drew back as if focussing on a memory that would not go away. "I was watching TV. I saw a Viet shoot a gook right in the head. He just fell down right there, the blood and all. He looked like a boy, his shirt hangin' out. It was like a man blew his own son away, like he did it to one of his own kind, himself. I thought that was weird, couldn't make no sense of it. You know what I mean?"

Yes. I too saw it over and over again.

"I mean the way he just fell down just like that. That's what was weird," Sam said. "Like he knew he had it coming to him and didn't have time to mind."

Sam got drafted for a year just like the rest of us, and he counted the days backward, one by one. He had a hundred and twelve days to go when he got hit, because we arrived the same day and I kept track too. Collins, the dope freak, and Boudreau, the Atlanta black, came a couple days later, and Thompson, the one who hated unions, was the greenhorn, the last to arrive. We were all in the same squad, buddies, though we didn't like each other very much. Sam, who if he cared about anything didn't seem to care one way or the other, was maybe why we hung together the way we did. So when he died it was like we lost the one we liked the most.

We had seen the dead before. We saw them carried in one by one, unloaded from a chopper or truck, and we heard stories too terrible to tell. The dead were here and gone, nameless unlucky ones. And the day we saw the truck—Sam saw it first—the truck loaded down with them, the bags, all zipped closed, piled right one top of each other as if they were full of leaves, we suddenly knew that this business we were in was bigger than all of us combined, that there was a lot we could not bother to take personally from then on.

We were sure Sam would be the one to get out of the mess alive, the one to shrug it all off, believe in the next thing that came along, move on. He was big, not like the skinny VC we knew were hiding out there picking on us. So when he got hit it wasn't just unfair. It was like seeing that truckful of dead men in plastic bags.

At first nobody said a thing, but everybody was quiet about it too long. Since I wasn't on the patrol when it happened to Sam, I thought I should be the one to start the talk. "What happened?" I whispered to Collins and Boudreau. "What happened to Sam?"

They just turned away at first, gave no more than dead stares. But one night I heard them talking low, and I heard Sam's name, and they were arguing.

The facts are the easiest part. "He just stood up," Collins said, "and he must've been loaded with Mary Jane because he walked right to the treeline where the VC were. Then bang, he went down. Dig it, man?"

"Why would he do a thing like that?"

"We wuz suppose to lay low," Boudreau said.

"You're all full of shit," Thompson said. "You make Sam sound like some crazy fool."

"All he drank was beer," Collins said. "He didn't dig the Mothers of Invention. So maybe he was a crazy fool, maybe he got high just once and it was too much for him."

Thompson looked at Boudreau, nodding his head as he spoke. "He didn't walk anywhere, except at first. Then he broke into a run, headed straight for the gooks."

"And that's why he got his Purple Heart," Collins smirked. "Right through the head. Dig it, man."

"Tell them, Boudreau," Thompson said as he pointed at me. "Tell Lund he didn't just walk."

Boudreau didn't look up. "They tol' me to lay low 'til the gunships come in. So I lay my head low. I didn' see nothin'."

"He started slow at first," Thompson said as he reviewed the scene, "like he didn't want to do anything weird, and then he picked up his pace, made a dash straight for the treeline, the chickenshit gooks."

"Then why did he turn and wave at us?" Collins asked.

"He wanted us to come on. He wanted us to follow him."

"Like a cowboy," Collins chimed.

"Oh shut up," Thompson said. "All of you goddamn pricks shut up."

And everybody shut up for more than a week.

Still the facts were the easiest part. I began putting them together one-by-one by asking a question here and there. Two hundred yards, the radioman said. The VC were in the woods; the platoon was on the low ridge looking down on them. Two hundred yards. Two hundred, no, two thousand years. The VC were there, but nobody saw them. And if every man crawled to within three feet, nobody would see one of them. Because nobody could see into the woods, and the woods ran on and on, deepening into a forest and the forest into a jungle that got so thick no sunlight would ever get through. And the trees in there had to be two thousand years old, and there had to be millions and millions of trees for VC to hide behind.

Everyone agreed that Thompson was the closest one to Sam just before he got hit, so Thompson had the most to say. "The funny thing," Thompson mused one night, "is that they told us the gooks would come running out after the gunships stirred them up in there. But nobody came out."

"Wuz you gonna shoot at the whites o' they eyes?" Boudreau asked.

"Maybe they went the other way—back where they came from. Them chickenshit gooks are like monkeys, you know. They go from tree to tree." Thompson had never seen, but he believed. "Had to be one up in a tree. Had to be a sniper up there looking through his sight right at Sam."

"The trees were two hundred yards away."

"Then from the grass. They lie in the grass, you know. I know a guy who almost stepped on a gook."

"I almost stepped on a goddamn snake last week," Collins said. "Pissed in my pants and caught a cold."

"The question," I said, "is what made him snap."

"Temporary insanity," Thompson announced. "He knew the chickenshit gooks were in the trees and he hated them. He kept everything

136

in and it was too much. So he suddenly snapped. He gets a sidearm out, and because he still hasn't lost his cool, he walks right at them to show them who's boss. He figures he can do it all alone, and he figures we'll back him on our own. He looks back to see if we're backing him, he waves for us to charge, then he loses his cool, runs at the trees, and bang, one of the chickenshit gooks nails him, blindsides him.''

"Zap." Collins looked up as if it were about to rain. "Led Zeppelin. The Jefferson Airplane. Do you dig?''

"What the hell's he talking about?'' Thompson asked me.

"He be fried in the brain,'' Boudreau shrugged.

It was hard for the brain to escape untouched. Sam and I had found that out. I was with the others in a bunker one night, all of us pulled in close, so I decided to tell them what happened to Sam and me.

"There were only six of us required to go. We were under Snabel—you know the one I mean, the one with the crooked nose, the sonofabitch who's all gung-ho. He said he was a miner's son and used to this kind of work—said he wanted a couple of tough farm boys for the job. That's why he took one look at Sam and said he wanted him, and Sam never had a chance to say he wasn't a farm boy, couldn't remember the time he lived on a farm. Anyway, we both had to go.

"It was early in the morning and there was a haze over everything up to our knees, so we couldn't see one foot in front of us. We didn't have to go far—about a mile from here.''

"You mean from here, the base?'' Thompson was more than alarmed. "You mean the commies have tunnels a mile from here?''

"I mean from here—up to the rise just south of here. Snabel told us to sit down and wait, and then as the sun rose higher in the sky and the mist began clearing out, we saw what we had to do. Because there were holes here and there—six of them in all—tunnels.''

"Those goddamn gooks are rats,'' Thompson said. He couldn't believe it. "You mean they had tunnels a *mile* from here?''

"Sure,'' said Collins, "who do you think cooks the food in the mess? They come in like elves every night, poison us a little at a time, and then sneak out.''

I could not tell them of the terror that shivered through me when I saw the holes—how I visualized the VC in there belly-down or curled up asleep, their hearts red with a wild fire stolen from the core of the earth itself, their eyes watching our every move, waiting for us to turn our backs so they could resume their slow relentless burrowing toward the place where we had built our barracks and beds, their arrival in silence and night from underneath to bring down the barracks like a heap of sticks.

" 'We got to go in there,' Snabel said. 'We got to go in there and root them out.' ''

"We all thought he was mad. We all looked around at each other like

137

we thought for sure he was kidding us, and I saw Sam look around for some way out, as if he would have run if there were some door he could slam behind him and leave it all behind, some . . ."

"Get on with the story," Thompson said. "That's the trouble with you, Lund. You always add bullshit to what you say."

"Snabel said there was only one way to be sure to get them out. We could torch the caves, drop grenades in, but there was no end to the holes—so we had to go in after them. We all looked at each other like he had holes in his head. 'You want us to go in *there?*' we said.

" 'You gotta do it,' Snabel said, 'or I'm gonna make life miserable for you.'

"Nobody volunteered so Snabel gave us a number. I was thee and Sam was four. We all had a tunnel to clear out."

Collins couldn't resist. "Thompson should've been in on that one. He's really into worming his way into yellow Saigon snatch."

"Shut up, you motherfucker."

"What Sam do?" Boudreau asked.

"What did we all do? We couldn't believe our eyes when Snabel crawled down the first hole. He went down head first, and when his feet disappeared it looked like he had been swallowed by a snake. He went down bit and loud, cursing the VC all the way to let them know he was coming in, maybe to scare them further in or out, maybe like whistling in the dark. 'When I give three yanks on the rope,' he told us, 'you guys start pulling me out. That means I went as far as I could go.'

"When he came out alright we couldn't believe our eyes. He backed out ass-first because there was no room to turn around inside. 'Nobody down there in that one,' he said with a big dirty smile on his face. 'Didn't think there would be.' So we all had to do what he did, then we'd blow the holes up."

"Dig it," Collins said.

"When Straughn—he was second—came out alright, we, Sam and I, were shitting in our pants. You know how it is. You figure they're lucky, so you'll get nailed for sure. I was shaking. 'Your turn next,' Snabel said. 'you gotta go in.' And for some goddamned reason I went in."

"What was it like?"

What was it like? It was like nothing. It was like dreaming about sleep. No, it was better, no, worse, than that. Because there was no light, and it was damp, and there was a smell like nothing else in the world. And I seemed to crawl forever and I never saw anything anywhere, and I didn't know if I was going in or down or around, then suddenly I was terrified and I yanked on the rope a thousand times, and my heart stopped until I felt them pulling me out.

So what was it like?

"Sam. Sam had to go next."

"I'm a city boy," Collins said. "Unqualified for that kind of work. No skills, no work. That's what the man says. All I want to do is make some music and go home."

"I think something happened to Sam down there," I began again. "I think that's when Sam snapped. No, not snapped. He started tearing apart. Like a rag, you know, that's been washed out too many times, how it begins just giving way."

"A gook? Did he find a gook in there?"

"He found something worse."

"Worse? What?"

He didn't back out the way we did. He came out head-first, from the same hole he went in. "Nothing."

"What do you mean nothing?"

"The holes had nothing in them. We just blew everything up. Then we went away."

I couldn't explain about the change that came over Sam. Maybe I was the only one to see the change because I was the one who saw his eyes when we pulled him out. He began staring at nothing in particular, as if he were drunk or on drugs. Then one day I caught him sitting alone in the sun. He had something cupped in his hand and he was stealing glances at it. I caught him in the act and made him face the fact. "The picture of the baby girl my kid sister had," he said. "I don't know why it had to be a girl. They look funny, don't they? I wonder when they open their eyes."

Later, inside, I found the picture in a wastebasket, all torn up. "Sam," I said, "why did you tear it up?"

"Because it gives me the creeps. Because it give me the creeps."

A few days later I had the courage to ask. "Was yours the same as mine? I mean the hole—when we had to go in?"

"It didn't go nowhere. It didn't go nowhere at all. I just kept crawling further and further in, and I couldn't see a goddamn thing. Not a goddamn thing."

He waited a long moment before he spoke again.

"And when I came out I couldn't see a goddamn thing. And here it was the middle of the day. I didn't know if I was coming or going."

His eyes showed more than confusion. He had been betrayed. "That Snabel," he said. "I can't figure why he made us go in. We didn't have to go in. We didn't have to."

"What could we have done?" For the first time I was aware that the order was absurd.

"We could've just blown everything up," he said as if he were asking me.

I shied away from Sam for almost a week after that, almost as if he carried a disease. Because he wasn't the same, everybody shied away from him, just as they refused to mention his name after his body was bagged, boxed and shipped to the States, the memory of him still too alive to allow us to believe he was gone, and the shame—a secret shame that it was he who got nailed and not us—too much for words.

But after that week Sam seemed to return from the dead. He was the one who told me we were getting a few days off in Saigon. Snabel arranged it all. "You boys got it coming to you," he explained. "Be good for you to get a breath of fresh air."

It was in Saigon, just outside one of those makeshift whorehouses where the girl stays behind a curtain and reaches out with a hand for a passing GI, that Sam got a new hat. He was wearing the other one when an old man came up to us from behind. He had a cart and a mule, asked us for money so he could go back home. Sam just pointed at the old man's head and said he wanted the hat. The old man was terrified, almost about to run, thought Sam was saying he was going to shoot him in the head right there on the spot. But when he finally calmed down he sold the hat to Sam—one of those regular hats shaped like a cone. Sam looked the hat inside and out, then took his cowboy hat off and stuffed it into his bag like a leftover hamburger he didn't know what to do with. He wore that hat everywhere in Saigon for the next two days, and I never saw the other one again.

The hat pissed Thompson off. "What you wearing a goddamned gook hat for? Some Joe's gonna blow your head off by mistake."

Still Sam wore the hat around the barracks, and he took to being more alone than ever before. Whenever he got a chance he sat under an old elm behind the messhall, the hat shading his eyes.

I sat down with him one afternoon, and from the middle of nowhere he had a question for me. "I've been wondering," he said. "Do you think the VC really live down in the holes?"

"That's what they say. They say that's where they go when the firefights begin—why we can't find any of them. They say the got whole cities down there. They make guns down there, and ammo and other stuff, and they've got their women and kids down there."

He shook his head in disbelief. "Goddamn," he said. "They're something, ain't they?"

Thompson couldn't get over Sam's new hat. "What did you do with the other one," he asked out of the blue. "Why don't you get rid of that goddamn thing?"

Boudreau was always alert when the whites fought among themselves, but he never said a word and his eyes were a little afraid.

"You running a union?" Collins asked Thompson. "You got membership cards for us, gonna charge us dues?"

"Blow it out your ass," Thompson said. "You and Lund can both blow it out your ass."

Collins broke into song. "Tum, tum, tum, tum. You gotta blow your mind."

"Shut up," Thompson said.

"Hey man, I gotta make my song. Dig it? I gotta find me a machine to make my song."

The week before we lost Sam, Collins went to Saigon for three days. He went all alone, without asking any of us.

The day after Collins got back we ran into an ambush less than a mile from the base. The VC popped up out of the ground behind us, right from the ground we had just covered, and then suddenly they were popping up everywhere, all around. We just hit the dirt.

"Goddamn, goddamn," Thompson screamed as held his helmet tight.

Boudreau was quivering uncontrollably.

"My machine," Collins yelled at Sam, "what a time to be without my music machine." And right in front of us he popped a small white pill.

Some Cobras saved us just in time. We heard their clapping behind the noise of the fire we were taking from all sides, and we would never be as happy as when we were sure they were coming our way. The VC went crazy firing just before the Cobras arrived. We could feel their fire searing the air just inches from our heads, and all we could do was flatten ourselves even more, dig at the earth with our nails to get closer, into it.

Then suddenly the fire stopped and we were left with only the clapping of the Cobras hovering beyond our view. And then we heard them distance themselves, fade into the sky, and suddenly we were left with only small sounds—the breeze sifting through the grass, the buzz of an insect here and there.

Boudreau was the first to dare lift his head. "What we do now?" he whispered.

"Somehow get back to the base," I said.

We looked around for Thompson. He was gone. We were too afraid to worry about him, too afraid to ask even with our eyes. We arose together on cue, hunched down as low as we could, and fanned out over the field. Then, looking everywhere around, we hurried back to the base, careful mostly of where we placed our feet, as if there were snakes everywhere in the grass.

Thompson was sitting alone when we got back. "When I heard the choppers leave," he explained, "I just beat it back home."

Boudreau turned his back and walked out.

"I'll say one thing. They're tough little niggers, them gooks." Thompson's eyes were amazed. "I'll say that for them."

In the corner I saw Sam shaking his head, yes, yes, yes, his eyes narrowed the way they were when he came out of the hole. Collins, sitting alone in a corner and swaying in rhythm to the beat of an invisible guitar, saw the look in Sam's eyes and had the decency to make no wise-ass remark.

It wasn't horror that appeared in Sam's eyes; nor was it simple fear. It was a new terrible understanding he didn't have words to explain. The others saw it too, wondered what the answer to the riddle was, but had no words themselves. And though they were afraid to speak, they knew that Sam would not simply abandon them, walk into an enemy bullet and leave them in the dark. So whatever it was he knew had to be expressed in fact or deed. It had to have everything to do with his suddenly standing up and walking toward the treeline where he knew the VC were waiting for us.

It was Thompson who finally broke the silence again. "I keep thinking about him. I keep thinking about the way he just stood up to them. I been thinking he has nothing to show for it, a guy that's a hero like he was."

"Dig it," Collins said as he turned his music down.

"It takes some kind of guts for a man to do what he did," Thompson went on.

"That's not why he did what he did," I said.

"Then why did he do what he did?" Thompson shot back.

"Because," Boudreau said, his eyes certain and wide, "because it wuz God hisself made 'em do wha' he did. He wuz struck down by the hand o' God."

Thompson nodded. That was not inconsistent with his view.

"That wasn't it," I said. "Not it at all."

"How do you know?" Thompson raised his voice. "You think you're so goddamn smart. Well Sam was a helluva lot smarter than you think he was. So how do you know? You weren't even there, Lund. You were safe and sound, right here, so how do you know?"

I didn't know but I was closing in on the truth. If anyone would have come with me I would have gone back to the scene, measured actual distances, groped in the weeds for some fact, some shard from which to piece together a picture we could all believe. And nothing less than belief is what we required. It wouldn't be enought to speculate, to go our separate ways thinking our own and very different thoughts about what happened to Sam.

"So what do you know?" Thompson persisted. "You weren't even there."

"I know what I know," Collins said. "I got my recording machine, and some night when the atmosphere's right I'm going to record me a concert like none you ever heard before. I'm just biding my time."

"We all bidin' our time," Boudreau said.

Thompson was right. I didn't really know. I didn't know if Sam was a Democrat or Republican. I didn't know what he really wanted out of life. I didn't know if he was afraid of anything—the VC, his mother or girlfriend back home, snakes. How then could I know what made him do what he did, if I was the one who believed that what a man does, his outcome, doesn't so much happen to him as it comes out of him? I didn't know for sure, but still I was closing in on the truth.

"Tell me one thing," I said to everyone in the room. "Tell me how many shots he fired at the VC."

Boudreau didn't lift his head, and Collins pointed a finger at Thompson. "He got one shot off," Thompson said.

"With his sidearm?"

"That's right."

"But if he was charging the VC, why didn't he open up with automatic fire?"

Nobody had an answer.

"Are you sure he got off one shot?"

"Sure I'm sure," Thompson said.

"And then he got nailed?"

"Just as he turned to wave goodbye," Collins said.

"Did you hear the VC shot?"

They all looked at each other. Finally Boudreau spoke. "I didn't hear but one shot."

"It was blam-blam just like that," Thompson said.

"Are you sure?"

"I'm sure, I'm sure. Blam-blam just like that."

The final proof came the following night. After midnight the VC had popped up out of their holes and were sending mortar rounds into the base from near and far and all around. Our own artillery was answering back, pumping thundrous round after round into the night, blindly blasting away at the grassland and forests no one could see. With our ears close to the ground we could hear the explosions miles away, the earth quaking with fear.

We were all in the dark, Boudreau, Thompson and I hugging the ground near the sandbagged wall, but Collins was wild with joy. "I'm getting it! I'm getting it!" he said as he darted around putting the microphone from his recorder against the walls as if he was measuring their breathing with a stethoscope. "I'm finally getting it all!" He had his machine, the tape recorder, turned up all the way. "Led Zeppelin and all this, all on one tape. And maybe Jefferson Airplane too, if the firing keeps going on!"

The silence followed as it always did, even Collins content to slouch in a corner with his eyes half-closed after the lights came on again. We had no good excuse to talk about Sam right then. Maybe it was some memory of the ambush that brought him back, some sense that we had been through that together and wanted him with us again. More likely it was something more, a sense that the war was too much to endure, that somehow he, even if too ignorant and unsure of anything to keep us together long, would somehow keep us from falling apart.

"It don't seem right being here without Sam," Thompson began.

"Another five minutes and I would've had it all," Collins complained in his corner to himself. "The whole Jefferson Airplane too."

Thompson was shaking his head. "For the life of me I can't figure out what happened to him."

"Don't you remember?" I said. "He was a hero. He charged the VC all on his own."

"I know, I know. But I can't figure out what made him decide to do such a thing. It was so nuts."

"Temporary insanity," Collins mumbled under his breath. "You just wait 'til I get my new headphones."

"It wuz God's will," Boudreau said.

I sidled up closer to Thompson. "What happened? You were talking to Sam just before he did what he did. What were you talking about?"

"Nothing. Nothing."

"What were his last words?"

"I could tell he was gonna do something stupid, I could just tell."

"What did he do?"

"He was wearing that goddamn gook hat. That's what he did. Here we were in the bush and here he was wearing a gook hat."

"What did you say?"

"I told him he'd get his head blown off. I told him to put his helmet on like the rest of us."

"And he wouldn't go along?"

"I told him what if one of our boys mistakes him for a gook? I made him get rid of it."

"Then he put his helmet on?"

Boudreau had heard every word. "No sir. He didn' have no hat on, no helmet neither, when he started walkin' up."

"Then he walked? He didn't charge?"

"Yes sir."

"Right at the end he charged," Thompson objected.

Collins suddenly stood up. "Right at the end, man, he said dig it. He said dig it, man, and he turned and waved at us. He didn't run nowhere at the end."

"Yes sir, he wuz struck down by the hand o' God."

"I don't understand," Thompson said, "why he couldn't go along with the rest of us, why he had to wear that goddamn gook hat."

"Did you see any snipers anywhere?" I asked.

"Just Sam, man, standing right up in front of us."

"Did he point his gun at anyone? Take aim?"

"Hey man, he just waved goodbye."

I tried to see Sam one more time, his blond hair shining in the Vietnam sun, the last gleam dancing off his perfect white smile, and the friendly hand waving goodbye to everyone, assuring us, just as he had assured his mother and father and sister at the airport for his last long flight, that there was nothing to worry about because everything was under control.

"And then you heard a shot?" I asked.

Collins nodded, while Thompson and Boudreau hung their heads.

"Then I know," I announced. "I know exactly what Sam did and how he died."

"Bullshit!" Thompson said. "Bullshit! You weren't even there! How would you know?"

"It wuz the 'rat o' God killed that po' boy."

"Bullshit! Now you all listen to me," Thompson said. "I know exactly what it was killed Sam. Now you all listen to me."

Yes, yes, we all said. You tell us now.

"Communism," Thompson said. "It was communism killed Sam."

That was the final word, because the lights suddenly went out and no one had the stomach to talk about it again.